# *here comes love*

## A PARALLELED LOVE
### BOOK 2

## BROOKELYN MOSLEY

85 MEDIA LLC

*Here Comes Love*
A Paralleled Love Series, Book Two
Copyright © 2026 by Brookelyn Mosley



This book is a work of fiction. Names, characters, places, and incidents either are products of the author's imagination or are used fictitiously. Any resemblance to actual persons, living or dead, events, or locales is entirely coincidental.

ISBN (eBook): 978-1-965507-64-3

ISBN (Paperback): 978-1-965507-66-7

**First Edition, 2026**

Published by 85 Media LLC

85 Media LLC

6614 Avenue U # 575

Brooklyn, NY 11234-6021

www.BrookelynMosley.com

- My First, My Last
- Envy
- Ready or Not
- So This is Love
- Home Before Midnight
- Gluttony
- When Luke Met Juliette
- When Life Gives You Sunsets
- In Love, I Trust
- Wrath
- Sloth
- Raising Love
- My Only
- How to Lose Control in 42 Days

### Short Stories

- Unsilent Knight
- Twice In Love
- Home For Christmas

# bybk exclusives

Bed Bully
Stuck
LHR Rewind Series
Home Before Midnight
Maybe This Time Will Be Different
Lovekilla
Incoming Call
Rough
WYD
Drinks on Me
Cali & Lee
Ray & Jay
Living Out a Love Song
Glimpses
One Mic
With Love, Ayanna & Dallas
Just Friends
Lena's Ex-File
Dream Boss

Chateau Luxure
Second Serving
Glimpses Vol. 2

*message from the author*

Thank you for purchasing your copy of *Here Comes Love*. This story is Book 2 in *A Paralleled Love* series. I encourage readers to read Book 1 before reading Book 2 for context. For deeper emotional context, I recommend readers read the bittersweet love story *Last Comes Love*, which *A Paralleled Love* series spins off from.

*Here Comes Love* follows Rylee Daniels as she heals from the loss of her best friend and the father of her two children, Lennox Walker. Other than scenes that capture her navigating through life while living with grief, there are no major trigger warnings to note.

Thank you again for purchasing your copy of *Here Comes Love*. I hope you enjoy reading Rylee's final book in my book world as much as I enjoyed writing it.

Love,

BK.

"LJ CALLED XANDER *DAD* LAST WEEKEND," Rylee revealed, her eyes on her therapist, Dr. Liz Peters. "And I haven't been able to breathe since. Not because he said it, but because LJ said it with so much ease. It's crazy for me to have that reaction, right?"

Rylee had rehearsed other ways to bring that up on the drive here —safer ones—but the truth always came out first whenever she had Liz in her sight.

Because so much can change in such a short time. Life can unfold in ways you never saw coming… and love, too.

Rylee Daniels knew that better than most. She sat comfortably in her therapist's basement office, that question lingering in her mind, refusing to let go. She knew the answer was coming, whether she liked it or not.

And that's why she loved it here. Liz's office encouraged Rylee to get lost in her thoughts and to never brush them aside. To analyze them, study them, even question them, and today she needed to do all of the above.

Rylee lifted the mug of hot coffee to her lips to blow into the cup. Her eyes settled on Liz, who'd just taken a seat in the chair opposite her, a smile already resting on her lips.

"What a way to start today's session," Liz started. "And already I can see the weight of that question lifting because you asked it. So to answer it in short, no it's not crazy."

Rylee exhaled a deep breath.

"It's good to see you, as always." Liz settled in her seat, setting her black notebook on her lap. "We'll get to what you asked in a moment. But before we begin, how are things?"

Rylee couldn't help but smile at the question.

Because aside from *that*, things were actually... perfect.

"Great." Rylee nodded, exhaling the deep breath she'd inhaled. "Really great. As you know, The Hope Collective is doing really well."

"*Mmm-hmm*," Liz answered with a nod.

"It's flourishing," Rylee continued, smiling. "We're almost too big for the bookstore basement in Cobble Hill." She focused up at the ceiling to gather her thoughts. "The kids are doing really well. LJ started preschool last September. And Nova's loving kindergarten but is not looking forward to first grade after I informed her there will be no more naps at school once she starts first grade."

Liz let out a soft giggle. "Honestly, I don't blame her for being hesitant to leave kindergarten. If I'd had the option, I might've stayed there myself."

Rylee laughed. "Oh, she is unsettled by that news."

It was Liz's turn to laugh.

"*Hmmm*... let's see... what else?" Rylee's eyes bounced around the office, soft sunlight beaming through the basement window, casting an unintentional spotlight over her. "Oh! Business is fantastic. I've been able to hire a couple of virtual assistants to give me more time to rest and relax."

"Very good," Liz responded, crossing her legs in her chair. "And *now* the boyfriend?"

If Rylee's brown skin were a few shades lighter, it would have brightened into a blush red. Instead, it glowed like the rest of her whenever Xander was mentioned or her mind wandered to thoughts of him.

"How's everything going with Xander?"

Rylee couldn't help but moan to herself, lift her mug once more to blow into it, hoping to hide her smile.

Rylee was in love. So in love... and feeling really guilty about it.

"It's going... well," she acknowledged with a slow nod. "Almost *too* well."

Liz arched a brow.

Rylee leaned forward to place the mug of coffee onto the wooden coffee table in front of her and didn't lean back in her seat, eyes fixed on Liz.

"Xander's great, except sometimes I feel overwhelmed by how available he is to me."

Liz tilted her head to one side, her cloud of salt and pepper tight curls moving that way.

Rylee sighed then added, "He pops up just about every evening and helps with everything. He's just... *there.* Not *all* the time because obviously he has 24-hour shifts at the firehouse. He's a firefighter—"

"Yes." Liz tried to ball her lips to hide her smile. "You've told me. Several times. Often nervously."

"Well..." Rylee snorted. "To me, it is a dangerous job even though Xander swears it isn't. Anyway..." She gestured with her hand next, as if she were physically moving that thought to the side for now. "He's not around all the time, but any free time he has, he's spending it at the brownstone and it's a lot. You know?"

"Okay," Liz answered. "And what about that feels wrong to you?"

"Oh." Rylee frowned. "It's not wrong. I didn't say it was wrong. Did I *say* it was wrong?"

"Your tone suggests you feel it is."

Rylee shut her eyes and sighed once more. "I know, I sound stupid—"

"You do *not* sound stupid."

"Well then this brings me to what I mentioned a moment ago." Rylee sat up in her seat. "LJ called him Dad the other day and my heart felt like it dropped out of my chest and hit the damn floor. Hard. So hard, I swore I felt the impact. I still feel it."

Liz nodded then lowered her gaze to her black book to jot something down.

"And... it was so unexpected. So out of the blue. I..." Rylee shook her head. "I've been so intentional with always reminding the kids who their father is. I keep photos of him in their bedrooms, in mine, around the house." Rylee lifted her arms and let them drop. "LJ didn't ask if he could call Xander Dad. He just... said it. *Dad*. Blurted it right out at the dinner table when asking Xander to pass the ketchup."

Rylee dropped her head into her hand, running her fingers through her long box braids.

"I just... I *love* Xander, and I love that my kids love him too, but..." She shook her head. "I need them to not love him like *that*. Because they already have a dad. He isn't here in the flesh, but they have one already."

It made no sense, loving how Xander loved them while wishing he wouldn't love them so much. Rylee knew that... but it was her truth.

Liz bobbed her head then lowered her attention to her notebook again to write in.

And Rylee giggled. "Oh come on now, Liz, don't do me like that."

Liz lifted her eyes to look Rylee's way, her pen still moving in her notebook.

"Don't give me the nod-and-write thing after I've said such a horrible thing."

"It isn't horrible," Liz corrected, placing her pen inside of the notebook. "I'm just noting progress."

Rylee furrowed her brows. "Progress?"

"Yes!" Liz beamed, nodding again, this time reassuringly. "Rylee, almost three years ago, you were sitting in that same chair across from me telling me you'd rather drink bleach than date. Do you remember that?"

Rylee exhaled a laugh while nodding her head.

"You refused to think about dating, which was completely understandable. But now..." Liz gestured at Rylee lovingly. "Now, Rylee, you have a partner who is present, loving, and not only committed to you but to your family, too."

Rylee finally leaned back in her seat, her back resting against the throw pillows on the cozy couch.

This was another reason she loved coming to therapy. Liz had a way with reframing things, never making Rylee see the terrible in her thinking but providing clarity for her to see things a different way.

And Liz was right. It wasn't long ago that Rylee rejected the idea of dating. She'd decided that getting into a relationship as a mother of two young children just wasn't in the cards for her. She'd inundated herself with work, family, friends, to fill the space romantic love would take up. And without even looking, she found someone who was perfect for her... except he was too perfect, and for someone so used to disappointment, Rylee wasn't used to perfect in her life.

"What you've told me," Liz continued, "isn't a problem at all. It's a new level of healing you've arrived to. This is fantastic, Rylee. Truly."

Rylee allowed a brief smile to pull at the corners of her lips, allowing Liz's words to play on in her head.

*This is fantastic.*

This is good...

Then why was her heart having the hardest time agreeing with that?

"Here's what I'd like for you to do," Liz started. "I want you to try documenting the moments that scare you and then the ones that soften you. In a notebook, and in one column, name your fear in detail. In the other column, name what Xander actually did. Doing it this way should help you put things in perspective instead of focusing on your fear of change. It'll help you separate your concern from what's really happening."

Rylee smiled, finally feeling the weight on her chest lighten a little.

Truthfully, she'd kept a lot of what she revealed to Liz to herself. To her, it just sounded so first-world—but in terms of love.

Great guy all around, but too great where she feared her kids would forget their dad... or worse, love Xander more.

Rylee exhaled at that, leaning forward to pick her mug up off the coffee table to drink.

"How does that sound to you?" Liz quizzed. "Do you think you can do that and we discuss it during your next session?"

"Yeah, let's do that."

"Great," Liz replied, turning the page in her notebook to add new notes.

As Rylee's gaze shifted to out the window, already creating an invisible column in her head of her fears and the things that soften her about Xander, Liz asked, "What is it that you really want now, Rylee?"

Rylee refocused on Liz.

"Now that you have the kids, the career, and the boyfriend who you've described as great," Liz continued. "What is it that Rylee wants now?"

Rylee sat with the thought for a beat then did a shrugging gesture with the sides of her mouth.

A flash of Lennox laughing at the kitchen counter in the brownstone flickered uninvited through her mind. Quick, sharp, gone... just like that.

Like him.

"Other than my best friend back?"

Liz gave Rylee her usual sympathetic soft eyes.

"Nothing," Rylee added. "For once, everything is perfect... all except for that."

* * *

Birds chirped outside the bedroom window—a familiar Saturday soundtrack in Brooklyn Heights. Most people were easing into the weekend. Rylee, on the other hand, was stuck in a silent panic, sitting on the edge of her bed.

Rylee loved the weekends for the opportunity to spend time with her kids... who she was worried about this a.m.

Nothing serious.

Only concerning.

That they would find Xander in her bedroom.

She sat at the edge of the bed, feet planted firm against her floor, battling worry and being turned on.

Her eyes were fixed on Xander as he towered over one of the sinks in her en suite, brushing his teeth. He lifted his head, pushing back the neat crown of dark brown locs that always seemed to fall into his eyes these days. His fade was still sharp, eyes even sharper when they met hers in the mirror.

He smiled over his toothbrush and winked, sending a surge of energy between Rylee's thighs that she wished he could do something about.

Because she wanted him to go... but she wanted him to stay too.

"You're taking forever in there," she teased, her eyes moving to her bedroom door. "You said to give you a minute and it's been almost five."

Xander chuckled to himself as he leaned forward to sip water to swish.

"How long does it really take to brush your teeth?" she continued. "It only takes two minutes for my teeth and maybe another minute for my tongue. You got an extra row in your mouth I don't know about?"

"Relax, Snoop," he advised, not bothering to look her way.

She rolled her eyes while balling her lips to keep from smiling.

His little nickname had grown on her. After almost three years of him not giving it a rest, it stuck, and as much as she tried to seem annoyed by it, she absolutely loved when he called her that.

Xander grabbed one of the face towels folded on the sink and turned to face Rylee.

There in just joggers, his torso sculpted obnoxiously perfectly, always beckoning Rylee's admiration without saying a single word.

"Happy, now?" he asked, turning his attention to the hamper in the en suite to toss the face towel into. "I'm done."

What she wouldn't give to just pull him back in bed with her to cuddle up and get cozy for a long morning in. Make a pillow of his biceps, drape her leg over his waist, close her eyes and get lost in his forehead kisses and back rubs.

But she couldn't. At least she's told herself she couldn't.

Her attention moved to the door before she was gesturing at him to keep moving.

"Cool, now get dressed."

She was up on her feet, lifting his firehouse-branded tee off a nearby chair and handing it to him.

"Damn." He chuckled, pulling his shirt over his head then poking his arms through the short sleeves. "You really got me feeling like you used me for my body and now you're kicking me out on my ass like you paid to play."

Rylee hollered a laugh then slapped her hand to her mouth.

She pointed at him. "Don't make me get loud."

He smirked, closing the distance between them. "Oh, you already did that last night."

She tried to escape his hug, but she was too late. Or maybe she kind of wanted to get caught.

As he wrapped his arms around her then bent his legs at the knees to press a kiss to her lips, her defenses slipped, one by one, and she had no qualms about it.

It's like Rylee told Dr. Liz, things had been great with Xander... too great.

He was an amazing man, with an even more amazing heart. He loved her, showed it, and extended that love to her children without hesitation.

It was that love for her children that made her nervous, though. They absolutely loved Xander.

Loved him a little too much, according to Rylee.

Xander moved his lips off hers to press sensual kisses against her neck, making her eyes roll closed. His big hand slinked down past her waist and over her ass to take a palm full in one grip, igniting a slow burn across her body.

She couldn't help the moan that left her lips, or the need to press her body even closer to his.

"Xander, *please*," she moaned, already losing resistance. The bed was right there. Just one lean back and she'd be his again. Return to making that good loving, the kind that extended from the night and into the morning to the point Rylee was tired but still hungry for more. "I don't want the kids to see you here."

He moaned against her, dragging his teeth up her jawline, making her shiver against him. "Would that be the worst thing?"

She sighed in defeat, wanting to speak but not wanting to leave that moment.

That indulgent moment of Xander wrapping her up in all the things her body was craving more of.

She opened her eyes to a photo of Lennox on her night table. A candid shot she'd taken of him, years ago, after they had Nova. He sat in the rocking chair that used to be in her nursery, cradling her. His long arms and big hands making Nova appear smaller than a basketball in his embrace.

And just as the guilt she'd tried her damndest to fight off started to set in, her bedroom door burst open.

*BOOM!*

"Mommy, Mommy!" Nova's sharp little voice pierced through the air. "Can we have—"

Both of her children gasped then squealed at the sight of Xander.

"Uncle Xander!" LJ shouted, running up to his mother and Xander, immediately jumping into Xander's arms.

Rylee couldn't help but both smile and ache at how Lennox Jr., who they all called LJ, wrapped his little arms around Xander's neck.

"What's going on, big boy?" Xander asked, hugging LJ then setting him down on his feet. He crouched down to be at level with LJ when Nova ran up to Xander, only stopping when her arms wrapped around his brawny shoulders, barely.

"I made a car at the home improvement store last weekend with my grandpa," LJ reported, his face beaming, smile fixed on his face. "Wanna see it?"

"Oh, I *have* to see it," Xander replied.

"Uncle Xander, can we make pancakes?" Nova asked next, her arm now resting on his shoulder in his crouched position in front of them.

"We gotta," Xander said with no hesitation. "What shape we making them into this time?"

"A star!" LJ shouted.

"A heart," Nova supplied.

"A heart and a star," Xander repeated, standing to his feet, the children's heads tipping back to keep their eyes locked on him. Xander extended both hands for them each. "Let's get to it. Who's cracking the eggs today?"

"Me, me," LJ and Nova replied in unison, their voices amplified and bouncing off the floors and walls.

Rylee stood behind them, completely left out of their huddle, but in complete awe at the sight of the three of them. She watched Xander and her children sink into their own worlds, laughing, talking in her bedroom.

He was so good with children, and it wasn't just because his mother owned a daycare and he was used to being around them.

He was just so good, period. At everything.

She watched as they held his hand and guided him out of the bedroom, not even glancing back once at their mother.

Her breath caught as she dropped herself back onto the foot of the bed and sighed.

"So much for you leaving before the kids get up," she mumbled to herself, shaking her head.

That was the only reason she let Xander in last night.

In that moment, she thought back to the night before, the moment this whole "morning problem" began.

*"Xander, what are you doing here?" Rylee whispered, peeking behind herself into the dark brownstone.*

*She'd just put the kids to sleep when she got the call from Xander letting her know he was out on her stoop.*

*He looked at her through his low-lidded gaze, bottom lip in the bite between his teeth. He extended his hand in front of him, caressed a finger down her tee. "Can I come in?"*

*Rylee rolled her eyes and fought back her smile. "You gotta stop just popping up like this."*

*He closed the space between them and pulled her closer to him by the hem of her shirt.*

*"I just put them to sleep."*

*"Perfect."*

*"No, not perfect." She settled into his arms as he wrapped them tight around her in her doorway. "You know I only like for you to stop by when they're at their grandparents."*

*"I needed to see you tonight, though." He leaned forward to press a kiss to her neck. "I needed to feel you too, Snoop. Badly, baby. Please."*

*She moaned into him, her arms wrapping around him before she could think better of it.*

*"I'll leave before they get up," he promised, kissing his way to her lips. On them he whispered, "I swear."*

So much for that.

He didn't even get up from sleep on his own that morning. To Rylee's surprise, he was still asleep when she awoke before him.

*With eyes barely opened, Rylee nudged him gently. "Xander... baby, get up."*

*He groaned.*

*"Uh-uh." She shook her head, bringing her fingers to her eyes to rub. "You gotta get up."*

*"Aight," he rasped. "I'm up, I'm up."*

*"Good, I'll be in the bathroom."*

*After slipping out of bed and taking a quick trip to her en suite to brush her teeth and freshen up, she returned to see he hadn't gotten up like he said he would. Instead, he'd turned off his stomach and onto his back, still asleep.*

*So, Rylee tried what she knew would get him up.*

*She pulled back the covers and stared down at Xander in the nude. One arm up over his eyes, masterfully sculpted physique making him look like a tatted Calvin Klein model in one of those 90s ads plastered on billboards.*

*"Xander," she called, her eyes locked in on perfectly dark coiled hairs around her favorite seat. "Xander."*

*No answer.*

*Rylee smirked, slipping in next to him again, but instead of relaxing on the pillow beside him, she grabbed his flaccidness, wasting no time guiding him into her mouth with one slow suction of her cheeks.*

*"Mmm," Xander moaned in his sleep. "Damn."*

*Rylee kept her eyes on him as she slid him in and out between her lips.*

*Eyes still closed, he found the top of her head, his hand landing on her braids that were gathered at her crown in a bun. He set the rhythm of her bobbing, pressing the back of his head into the pillow beneath him, his mouth falling open a second later.*

*"Mmm, baby, baby, Yesss."*

*Rylee smiled on his growing erection, abruptly sliding him free from her mouth. "Now, get your ass up."*

*"Yooo!" Xander laughed, grabbing the pillow she slept on to cover his face and groan into. "You're so foul for that."*

Rylee kissed her teeth and dropped herself flat onto the mattress.

Her head fell to the side, eyes landing that way and glimpsing the photo of Lennox on her night table.

She'd intentionally kept his photos in just about every room of the house. It was important to her that her kids knew who Daddy was. To her, it was the least she could do.

From upstairs she could hear their laughter and conversation down in the kitchen, and her heart ached.

This was good, this was supposed to be good.

Then why wouldn't her heart agree?

She rolled over on her stomach and took Lennox's photo off the night table, placing it on the bed within view.

"Things are changing, Lenny," she spoke to the photo. "I'm sorry."

She sucked her teeth and dropped flat onto the mattress, pressing the framed photo to her chest, hugging it.

Xander felt so right in her home, even righter with her children.

If only her heart would catch up to that fact.

RYLEE

"I VISITED CARTER'S GRAVE YESTERDAY," Trinity, one of the members, started, a small smile pulling at her lips. "I know it's a tiny step—"

"That's a *huge* step, Trinity," Rylee assured, nodding and holding a warm smile on her lips. "Major."

Rylee remembered the first time she visited Lennox's grave after his funeral. It was much sooner than Trinity. His gravestone had not been placed yet since the soil was unstable. But it was the spot they'd lowered him into, so she knew he was there. And she'd always remember the clench in her chest, the weight of the silence. It wasn't a small thing.

Trinity released a little laugh then inhaled a deep breath. "I haven't been to it since the funeral two years ago."

Rylee nodded once more.

"But something in me said, *just go, Trinity*. You know?"

"I know *all* about that little voice," Eden, another member, voiced. "Once it starts, you can ignore it but for so long."

"Until it becomes all you can hear," Rylee added.

And everyone released a variety of reactions, all in agreement.

It was a cold Sunday morning in Brooklyn, but the temperature in the Cobble Hill bookstore's basement was warm and cozy.

Between tall shelves of books lining every wall, the windowless room felt more like a safe haven than anything or anywhere else.

Which was Rylee's goal.

Candles flickered on intentionally placed small tables. Their soft glow mingled with the scent of vanilla, old books, and paper cups filled with coffee or chamomile tea that lingered like special guests in the air.

It was familiar and a signature of The Hope Collective meetings.

It was Rylee's contribution to the community of people who had lost partners and spouses to brain aneurysms. They'd meet every other week in the bookstore's basement, sit within the circular armchair layout Rylee intentionally created at the guidance of her therapist, Liz Peters, who popped in on the group every so often. And the group members would speak their truths. Share their experiences on how they were coping with their losses, offer up resources that helped them on their lifelong healing journeys they never knew they would ever have to embark on. Tears were shed. Comfort was given. It was a safe space.

The group members often thanked Rylee in tears for putting the group together, stating that without it, they weren't sure how they'd go on.

But what they didn't know, and that she often told them, was that they were as much help to her healing as she was to theirs.

"Anyone else wanna share something?" she asked, her beautiful brown eyes moving about the space, landing on everyone present.

"Yeah," the deep voice emerged to Rylee's right. "I do."

And when she glanced that way, her eyes came to rest on another group member. Yusuf Baldwin.

Yusuf had joined not long after his wife, Parris, passed. She'd had a surgery that had gone wrong, one he hadn't wanted her to take. Grief clung to him like a second skin back then, and he credited the group for helping him to not only cope with the loss but to continue on with life.

"Please, Yusuf, go ahead."

Yusuf smiled, then ran his hand down the top of his head.

"So... *umm...*" He chuckled nervously. "After I'm done here, I'm going to stop by my girlfriend's place to let her know about a trip I've got planned."

Rylee smiled at that, her deep dish dimples dotting her cheeks.

She remembered the day Yusuf returned from a trip to Hawaii, one he took to spread his wife's ashes. He not only returned happier, he'd brought back a souvenir that was life-changing... a new relationship.

"So as most of you know," he started, "when I flew to Maui in 2023, to spread my wife Parris's ashes, I met someone."

Everyone nodded.

"And... things have been great since then," he added. "She's amazing and is so understanding of my heart and my love for Parris."

Rylee crossed her legs to lean more in Yusuf's direction.

"So, this trip we're going on, which will be the first trip we've taken together since Hawaii, isn't just a trip."

Rylee's brows wrinkled as she tilted her head to one side.

"I'm gonna ask her to marry me."

Everyone in the room gasped or released sounds of enthusiasm.

Rylee's jaw simply dropped.

"What?!" she whispered, a smile soon tugging her lips up. "Shut up."

The room erupted in laughter, Yusuf joining in.

He nodded, his face completely brightened by the huge smile now taking residence on his lips. "Yeah."

All Rylee could do was clap in that moment, and the rest of the group members joined in.

"Thank you." Yusuf pressed a hand to his chest. "I appreciate you all, sincerely."

The applause gradually faded.

"This group," he continued, his hand still to his chest as he closed his eyes briefly. "It really saved me."

Tears pricked the corners of Rylee's eyes as she mirrored him, pressing her hand to her chest.

"Honestly?" he chuckled. "I didn't think love was in the cards for me. I thought Parris was it, and I thought I'd be fine with that, you know?"

The group members replied with nods or verbal agreements.

"But..." He gestured around the room. "You all encouraged me to fulfill her final wish, and I remember being so mad at y'all for that."

Everyone laughed softly.

"And if I would've ignored you all, decided that I wanted to continue to hang on and not honor Parris's wishes, I don't think I would have met my girl, Clarke. I don't think I would feel like life had any meaning or incentive to go on. Because beyond wanting to start a life with her, I just want to keep living. And I hope for anyone else here who was feeling like I was feeling, that you get to here, too." He nodded. "Not aiming for a new relationship, but just finding that desire to live again."

His words settled on Rylee's heart.

This is exactly what she meant when she explained that she healed just as much in their group meetings as they did by simply sharing their stories and experiences.

She was one of those people who had found love again. The only difference is that every time she felt herself moving out of the life of grieving Lennox, it scared her.

Made her feel like she wasn't honoring his legacy.

The promise she made to him.

That she would wait... until they were together again.

After more group members shared their stories and what they'd been experiencing since the last group meeting, it was time to wrap up.

There were hushed voices as everyone collected their things to head out.

As soon as everyone was up and out of their seats, Rylee was heading for Yusuf.

Close, she playfully punched him on his arm, and he laughed.

Yusuf had become someone like a brother to Rylee. Her most stubborn group member who refused to open up his first few visits to The Hope Collective group meetings.

Rylee tried everything to get him to share his story. He'd show up every other week and just sit silently, visibly holding a lot on his heart. And when he finally opened up, Rylee took a liking to him and his love for his wife, Parris. It reminded her a lot of her love for Lennox.

"Now, how you just gonna drop something like that in here?!"

Yusuf tipped his head back and laughed, his beautiful smile brightening the room.

He was happy, and Rylee noticed this happiness the day he attended the meeting after his trip to Hawaii.

"Yusuf, what?"

"I know."

"This is amazing," she whispered, taking him by his biceps. "So amazing!"

Group members made their way around Rylee and Yusuf, saying their goodbyes with promises to see them the week after next.

"So... how did you get here?" She threw her hands up. "I know you didn't go into details during the meeting, and I hope you don't mind sharing—"

"You know I don't mind sharing any of this with you, Rylee." He nodded toward her. "You're one of the reasons I'm even considering this to begin with."

She made an exaggerated pouty lip expression. "Aww."

He chuckled, pushing his hand into his jeans pocket.

When he pulled it out, he brought in his grip a ring box. A beautiful royal blue velvet square.

He flipped the lid, and Rylee's eyes grew at the sight of the diamond tucked in the slit.

"Oh, my *God*," she expressed low before looking up at him. "It's beautiful."

"Like her," he agreed, his attention fixed on the stone. "She picked it."

"*She* picked it?!"

He nodded. "I rented out a jewelry store months ago for her to window shop. Told her that I wouldn't ask her then, but I did want to make sure when I did, she loved the ring and it fit."

"Genius." She smiled.

Rylee inhaled a deep breath and let it out through her mouth.

"How do you know?"

Yusuf was returning the ring box into his pocket when he refocused on her.

"How do you know when you're ready?" she added. "I'm not trying to make you second-guess anything. I'm asking for myself... and maybe being a little selfish, if I'm honest."

He snorted a laugh.

"Because I've been in my relationship, as you know, and he's perfect not just on paper but just period."

"Yes, I know. You tell us every meeting."

She giggled. "But like... I don't know if I will *ever* be ready for this step, so *please* tell me. How did you know? Are you not a little scared?"

*Hesitant?*

She doesn't ask that extension to her question out loud.

"Oh, I'm terrified, Rylee. Look at my hand right now." Yusuf held out his hand, and it was shaking a little.

And as simple as it was, seeing that was somewhat of a relief.

"Even just the thought of asking Clarke is scary," he continued. "When I proposed to Parris, to me, that was it. I felt like I'll never have to get down on one knee again, nor would I want to. Forever. Period."

Rylee bobbed her head up and down. "Right."

"But then I met Clarke," he said. "And after a short time, I realized she was amazing, too. She wasn't Parris, and that was perfect, because Clarke was herself. And me not constantly trying to find Parris in life when she'd already died was a step that was hard to take. But Clarke..." He shook his head in awe. "She makes me look forward to new days. She understands my past, understands how it is a part of who I am, my story, and she accepts it all. She loves it all. So..." He shrugged this time. "I want this. And even though it's scary, I'm willing to do it scared with her because I know there's something beautiful on the other side of what scares me."

"Yeah," Rylee whispered. To him. To herself.

"Well, go ahead," she told him, pressing a hand to his arm. "Go to Clarke and tell her about this amazing trip that will be better than she'll imagine. I'm so happy for you, Yusuf."

She extended her arms, and Yusuf leaned into a hug with her, holding her tight.

"Thank you, Rylee," he told her, pressing a kiss to her cheek.

And she smiled at that.

"Thank *you*," she said, holding him tightly.

She pulled away from the hug, smiling. Because deep inside, something cracked open... not in pain, but in possibility.

Could she get to this place, too?

Could she stop waiting... and start living?

## three

### XANDER

BACON SALTING the air smelled like a good Saturday morning in Brooklyn. The sizzle of turkey bacon in the pan competed with the high-pitched voices of LJ and Nova as they spoke over each other between bursts of laughter.

And God, there wasn't a sweeter sound to Xander.

Well... actually, Rylee's moans were definitely—

"Can I, Uncle Xander?"

Nova's voice cut through his thoughts. Xander turned to look at her over his shoulder.

She stood near the dove gray marble counter, eyes fixed on him.

Nova had grown so much, and he was grateful to have witnessed every bit of it. Still, he missed the days when she used to call him *"Dander"* and sometimes wished her mother had never corrected her. The thought made him snicker.

"Can you what, Princess Nova?"

She giggled, her face lighting up just like her mother's did when she laughed.

"Stir the pancakes?"

She was already bouncing on her little legs, and because he could never say no...

"You absolutely can, your highness." He smiled. "The moment I put the batter together, it's all yours."

"Yes!" She pumped her fist in the air in celebration.

"But *I* wanna stir it," LJ chimed in, folding his little arms over his chest and pouting.

Xander stepped away from the stove, squatting beside him.

"Well, LJ, if you're over there stirring," he said, "who's gonna crack the eggs for me?"

LJ's face lit up.

"I gotta see if you were paying attention the other day when I taught you how to crack them the right way."

"Yay!" LJ shouted. "Cool!"

Xander held out a fist for him to bump, and LJ accepted.

As he returned to his full height, his eyes met Rylee's from across the kitchen. She was leaning against the wood-paneled entrance, her expression a mix of humor and something else... annoyance?

When he'd shown up at the brownstone that morning, on his day off, she hadn't looked too pleased.

*She'd sighed the second she opened the door.*

*"Didn't we talk about this?"*

*He handed her a paper cup of coffee from her favorite spot down the block, lifted the bag of groceries in his other hand, and leaned in to kiss her lips.*

*"I was in the area and thought I'd take making breakfast off your hands."*

*She closed her eyes and exhaled. Her lips parted to say more, but Nova's voice interrupted.*

*"Uncle Xander, yay! LJ, Uncle Xander's here."*

*Xander winked at Rylee and stepped over the threshold. She stepped aside to let him in.*

*"Uncle Xander's here," Xander teased, stealing another kiss from Rylee.*

Since then, she'd been giving him subtle death stares from across the room.

It had been almost three years since they made things official. He loved that woman and loved his time with her. But his time with her kids? That was unmatched.

They were amazing. He'd known that from the moment he met them at his mother's daycare during the week they stayed at Future Seeds Daycare. Since then, he'd been at every birthday, every school event, even helped them sell holiday candy, taking the catalogs to work and bullying his firefighter crew into buying holiday tins.

He might as well have *Dad in Training* tatted on his forehead.

And while the thought was a mix of pride and nerves, Rylee's constant reminders to *chill about it* took some of the wind out of him.

Like now... her arms folded, that too-tight smile she gave the kids when they pulled her into their bubble.

He turned the fire off beneath the last strips of turkey bacon and plated them.

"Aight, LJ." He lifted the boy onto the wooden stand Xander bought for the children last year when they first showed interest in helping him cook. It helped them reach the counter and made them feel like grown-ups. It was cute.

"I'm gonna leave these here with you," he said, tapping the closed carton of eggs. "I want you to crack eight."

"Eight eggs?!" LJ looked excited and nervous all at once.

"Eight eggs, big boy," Xander confirmed, tapping LJ's belly playfully. "You got this."

"Okay..."

"Let me hear you say *I got this*, Young Prince."

LJ puffed out his chest. "I got this."

"Aight!" Xander laughed. "So go 'head, crack them in this bowl. Try to keep the shells out, but if they get in there, it's cool." He pressed a hand to his chest. "Uncle Xander will help you fish them out."

"Cool!" LJ shouted, already reaching for an egg.

Xander turned to Nova. "Let's get the pancake batter together so you can mix it up, Princess."

She did a little dance on her way to the bowl that made him laugh out loud.

He loved this—being here, in their world, soaking up their energy.

And he thought Rylee was warming up to it too.

But every chance she got, she tried to cool it down.

He understood why. And yeah, it still stung.

Nova was stirring batter when Rylee moved past him to toss her empty coffee cup in the trash. He stepped behind her, pressing his hands to the counter on either side of her, caging her in.

"You gonna tell me I make better pancakes than you again?"

"No," she replied flatly, turning in his arms to face him. "I'm gonna tell you not to pop up anymore... again."

He leaned back slightly, a little stunned. But he forced a smile, pecked her cheek, and buried his face in her neck.

That pulled a giggle out of her before she pushed him away.

He tried not to take it personal. He hadn't planned this—hadn't meant to fall for her or her babies. But once he did, everything just fit.

Her. Her kids. This life.

How the hell was he supposed to ignore that?

"Aye." He caught her arm gently before she could walk away. "I'm sorry, okay? I was in the area on my day off, and I just wanted to chill with y'all this morning."

She sighed and whispered, "Which makes me a total *bitch* for even fussing about it, Xander."

"Aye, yo," he whispered back, flicking her lip playfully with his fingertip. "Don't you *ever* call my girl a *bitch*. Are you crazy?" He stepped closer, lowered to her level. "You want problems with me? You tryna square up? What's up? What's good, shorty?"

She tossed her head back laughing, then pushed him again.

"I did it!" LJ announced. "No shells!"

"Perfect!" Xander clapped. "I knew you could do it. I'll be over there in two minutes."

Rylee's voice came low. "The kids are getting too comfortable."

Damn. She really said that. Out loud.

It burned. But he knew better than to push. She wasn't there yet.

He furrowed his brows. "Too comfortable with what? Being loved, Snoop?"

She blinked quickly, then squeezed her eyes shut. Her hands slid down her face and dropped to her sides. "I just... I don't want them thinking you're their daddy."

He stepped forward and wrapped his arms around her waist. "They won't, aight?"

"LJ called you—"

"And I corrected him, right?" he reminded, recalling that dinner table moment. It had warmed his heart. But Rylee's panic had been so sharp, he'd quickly shifted—told LJ he loved being called Uncle Xander and that anything else would break his heart.

Truthfully? He'd loved it.

But clearly, she hadn't.

His eyes drifted over her shoulder, landing on a photo in the hallway. Lennox. The kids passed it every day like seeing their dad in a frame was nothing. And maybe that was the problem. They were constantly reminded of him. They weren't forgetting... but they were letting Xander in.

Why couldn't she let them let him in?

"They know who their daddy is," he promised softly, returning his eyes to her. "They really do. Don't even worry your pretty self about that."

She let out a breath, sharp and heavy.

"But you know..." he added, tightening his hold, "I can be your daddy."

She cringed, nose scrunching, lips twitching. "*Ew.*"

He laughed, and she did too.

But his chest? It was tight. So damn tight.

Would it be so bad to step into that role?

He wouldn't mind. He wanted to.

But Rylee didn't.

They finished cooking breakfast and gathered at the table. The kids did most of the talking. Rylee and Xander only got a few words in.

Every so often, she'd glance at him. Her eyes would soften. Her smile would almost come through.

It was moments like that that made him believe she might be warming up to the idea of this. Of him.

But then she'd say stuff like earlier.

*"I don't want them thinking you're their daddy."*

Well, damn.

Her words clung to him long after she spoke them, looping through his mind as he cleaned up after breakfast. Even while loading the dishwasher, wiping down the counters, and getting the kids to help—which they loved—he couldn't shake the sound of her voice.

An hour later, he still didn't want to leave.

If he had it his way, the kids would drift into their Saturday morning routines—TV, puzzles, dolls—and he and Rylee could curl up on the couch, do nothing, just be.

But he knew better. Suggesting that might send her into a silent panic.

So he gathered his things, hugged the kids, and headed for the door. Rylee followed behind.

He turned at the door, pulled her into a hug and a kiss.

"I didn't mean to overstep," he told her. "I want you to know that, okay?"

She smiled and nodded.

"It's a good thing I didn't decide to use that key you keep under that fake rock when you took too long to answer the door. Then you would've really been mad at me, huh?"

She gasped. "How do you know about that key?"

He smirked. "Spotted it when I was throwing out trash a month ago. Kicked the rock by accident. Noticed the key under it.

Which, by the way, that's a terrible place to keep a spare, baby. Terrible."

"Yeah, yeah." She rolled her eyes playfully. "After losing my keys years ago at a Mommy and Me meetup in the Botanical Gardens, I've been keeping them there. It works for me, so hush."

"*Mmm-hmm.*" He tapped her chin, tilted her head back, and kissed her again.

"What I wouldn't give to take you upstairs and work off all these pancakes and syrup, though."

She giggled, then moaned softly, arms tightening around his waist.

He ran his thumb along her lips. She opened her eyes, and the look in them did things to him he didn't need happening right now —especially since he couldn't act on them.

"I'll text next time," he promised, caressing her cheek.

He left a kiss on her forehead, opened the door, and stepped out onto the stoop.

At his truck, he leaned forward, behind the steering wheel, to peer through the brownstone window. He hoped to catch a glimpse of her, or the kids. But he couldn't see anything.

Xander had been finding it hard to fight the pull of wanting them under the same roof one day. It would be crazy to ask Rylee and the kids to move into his one-bedroom, but with Rylee drawing invisible lines he tried hard not to cross, it was hard for him to envision her home as his home too. Lennox's presence lived in those walls, and Xander respected that, even when it made him feel like a permanent guest in a life he wanted to be part of.

But a conversation that the firefighters at his firehouse were having over lunch weeks prior had been playing on repeat in his mind.

"*Aye, yo, have y'all heard that Greene Gardens is offering priority housing to first responders?*"

*Xander peeked up from his mac and cheese to focus on his fellow firefighter, Colt.*

*"You get price cuts, low-interest loans, the works,"* Colt said through his stuffed mouth. *"Brooks from Ladder 181 just bought a property out there."*

*"Word?"* Xander asked. *"How he like it?"*

*"Oh, he loves it over there,"* Colt replied, shoveling more food into his mouth. *"His house is huge. The neighborhood good too."*

*"Hmph,"* Xander replied, returning to eating. *"That's dope. Maybe I'll look into it someday."*

But the thought hooked in deep. A place big enough for the kids. A neighborhood that felt safe. A chance to build something of his own for the first time in his life.

It was just a thought.

A thought that wouldn't leave him. Especially not on that day as he sat in his truck, prepared to start it up and drive off... even when he really didn't want to. There wasn't a place he wanted to be more on that cold Saturday morning than in there, with them.

And he thought he was doing everything right to earn that place —being present, being gentle.

So why did it always feel like he was crossing a line trying to make a home with Rylee and her kids?

RYLEE

"AM I THE ASSHOLE?" Rylee asked, lowering her mimosa to the table with a soft clink. "Because really hear me out on this."

Rylee's friend Parker pursed her lips while her other friend Nadia sipped her drink and focused in on Rylee.

"So, *boom*," Rylee started, turning to face her friends in her chair. "I know I should be happy, right? This is what I wanted and what I thought I couldn't have but got anyway, right?"

"*Mmm-hmm*," Parker hummed with a nod.

"Right," Rylee continued. "And I'm not trying to sound ungrateful or whatever, but he just keeps popping up. He popped up again last Saturday saying he wanted to take breakfast off my to-dos and make it himself..."

Nadia peeked over at Parker at the same time Parker looked to Nadia.

"And you know..." Rylee cleared her throat. "I know how it *sounds*, but really see it a different way."

"Well, shit, friend, I hope where we're going with this gets bad at some point," Nadia started. "Because yes, you seeming like the asshole so far. Yes."

Parker giggled.

"The kids," Rylee began this time, tapping the table, rattling the glasses a little. "I'm worried about Nova and LJ."

Her friends' brows wrinkled.

"They get so damn excited when they see him and don't ever want him to leave to go home. LJ done called the man *Dad* because he loves him *so* much."

The quiet part to her rant was that Rylee wondered what that would mean for the man who should've had that place in LJ's heart. Her son had never met his father, so she feared Xander was slowly taking that place, erasing the memories Rylee had intentionally planted to fill Lennox's absence. Would those memories she worked so hard to make matter remain if she and Xander kept going?

Nadia kissed her teeth and raised her hand just as their waiter was walking past. "Can I please get another glass? And feel free to go light on the orange juice and heavy on the champagne because my friend here is getting on my damn nerves."

Rylee gasped.

"I'll take that same mix too," Parker echoed. "And for the same reason."

Their waiter chuckled. "Right away. I'll be back in a few with your refills."

"You hoes," Rylee uttered low, making her friends burst into laughter.

It was Brunch Sunday for the ladies. A once-in-a-while occurrence that hadn't happened since last summer. Between their jobs and Rylee juggling her business and her grief support group with motherhood, the only way these ladies had managed to catch up had been in group chats and FaceTimes between appointments.

That Sunday, they promised they'd meet up, even if only for an hour. Now, three hours and nearly five mimosas later, Rylee finally felt comfortable enough to get off her chest what she'd been holding in for months...

That Xander was amazing, and his amazingness was starting to make her worry.

"He made pancakes... again," Rylee added once they were alone. "With custom pancake shapes. And the syrup he brought... I didn't even know they had that kind of syrup—"

"My love," Nadia cut in, scooting to the edge of her seat. Over her shoulder, and through the thick pane glass window, the New York City skyline beyond the East River reflected the winter sunlight off the several glass fixtures that shaped the landscape. "Maybe you've forgotten what dating is like out here, and I feel it's my obligation to give you a quick reminder."

"Hello!" Parker added.

"But before I do that, let's recap what you've told us this afternoon." Nadia held up her hand and started using her fingers to count off. "The man cooked for your kids and didn't leave you with the dishes, cleaning them himself. The children love him so much that they would prefer he stay instead of leave, every time. Is that correct so far?"

Rylee sighed, tossing her braids off her shoulder and reluctantly nodded.

"He loves you, caters to you, is mindful of your heart and your needs," Nadia added. "And though you won't confirm, I can tell by the way you are glowing, he's taking care of you in bed."

Rylee rolled her eyes. "Would you get to the damn point, please!"

"Sure. Rylee?" Nadia placed a hand on Rylee's hand. "What you have given us are not problems. What you have explained to us is the answer to a *gahdamn* prayer."

"Okay!" Parker shouted, tossing back the last of her mimosa as the server brought their refills. "A prayer I'd like written on paper, word for word, bar for bar, because my ass need some grace and guidance out here. Shit."

"Thank you! And that brings me to my original point," Nadia jumped back in. "I'm a marketing exec and I had to make a burner account to find a halfway decent man on the damn app I work for. Me! Girl, dating out here, at least for me, is awful. Really, really awful, which I *know* you already know, Rylee."

"I do," Rylee mumbled.

"I mean," Parker chimed in. "And if it ever did slip your mind, you could always just remember that you were the same one who got dumped by email once upon a time."

Rylee blinked hard. "Oh! So the mimosas got your lips loose now? Girl, you better find something safer to do, Parker, 'cause this ain't it."

Parker laughed. "I'm not trying to trigger, just reminding you of something you may have forgotten."

Rylee sucked her teeth. "Now how would I *forget* something like *that*, Parker?!"

Parker motioned to Rylee. "*How* could you be here complaining about an amazing man?"

Rylee sighed once more and sat back in her seat.

She couldn't help but feel no one understood the position she was in... not even her close girlfriends.

Because yes, Xander was great. Amazing. But he challenged her norm.

A norm she worked really hard to get to.

The normal that had her best friend and father to her children's memory locked in place, and his spot never to be filled.

But here was Xander, not only filling the spot but making her and her kids happy.

And it was becoming a new normal, one she feared she'd forget Lennox in.

Or worse, possibly leave him behind to truly be in.

The mimosa buzz was warm in her chest, but the ache underneath refused to lift.

She poked at her food, her appetite long gone.

"Sometimes..." Rylee shared low, pausing to twist her lips to one side, taking a breath. She mindlessly pushed around her leftover chicken and waffles with her fork. "Sometimes I can't help but to think about what Lennox would say."

Those wrinkled brows belonging to her friends suddenly relaxed.

"I just... I know he's watching. He used to always tell me that tired ass line of when the clouds part and the sun's rays rain down on me..."

She stopped to smile to herself, her chest aching just a little more with that memory.

"I wonder if he'd be okay with it. If he'd like Xander."

The table was quiet, her friends listening.

It was the quietest they'd been since they arrived several hours ago.

"Like I know he'd like him." She smiled to herself, lifting her attention and only realizing she was crying when a tear escaped her watering eyes.

"Xander would probably have been the first guy Lennox *ever* approved of."

The ladies laughed softly.

"But I just..." She swiped a finger beneath her eyes, shrugged, and sat back in her seat. "Wonder. And that's literally all I can do. You know?"

Nadia scooted her chair closer to Rylee and took her hand. "Lennox is probably up there silently thanking Xander for not letting you crumble... if we're keeping it real, Rylee."

Parker nodded, picking up the napkin to dab at Rylee's eyes.

Rylee sniffed back her tears, gently taking the napkin from Parker to continue drying her eyes herself.

"And for real, Rylee," Nadia continued. "You're still honoring him. You're raising your children to know who he is. Reminding them of how amazing their dad was. But babe, you *have* to understand that you are allowed to keep living."

"Yes." Parker nodded. "And you're allowed to not feel guilty about that. Because that is the *last* thing Lennox would want. I don't know too much, but I *know* that much."

Rylee nodded too, really wanting to believe that.

Xander was exactly what she wanted but believed she wouldn't have.

And because she believed she couldn't have it, she stopped wanting it... only for it to show up to her with ease.

Maybe too easily?

The abundance of good things had made Rylee suspicious... and curious about finding out when the next shoe would drop.

The conversation didn't resolve anything for Rylee, but it did make it clear that she had been pushing Xander away... and it had been hard for her to do.

*Maybe I am making it harder than it has to be,* she thought to herself.

"Okay, okay," Nadia voiced, drying her eyes and sniffing back her tears. "We gotta lighten things back up. We can't be ruining our mascara like this."

Parker smiled, and Rylee laughed through her tears.

"Let's make a toast to the man who won't give up on our girl..." Nadia said, raising her glass, Rylee and Parker joining her. "Even when she makes it a damn Olympic sport with no damn medal to show for it."

Rylee rolled her eyes but laughed along with Parker.

She met her glass with her friends in a toast, and she flashed her signature winning smile... but deep down, her warring feelings still chimed louder than the clink of their glasses.

* * *

Later that evening, just as Rylee was straightening up the brownstone's living room, she heard her doorbell ring followed by a knock on the door.

It was a few minutes to 9 p.m. and she wasn't expecting anyone.

But considering how things had been as of late, she knew who it was.

Xander.

She shut her eyes and inhaled a deep breath. Glanced at her children playing with their Legos on the living room's area rug before making her way to the front door.

She'd planned to put the children to sleep after vacuuming, so a part of her was feeling some kind of *way* about Xander popping up... yet, again.

She peeked through the peephole and immediately unlocked the door. When she opened it, she was prepared to see that cunning grin on Xander's lips and to hear him beg her to come inside next, but both his smile and his words were missing.

His bomber jacket was unzipped, and he only wore a white tee underneath. Joggers wrinkled, face with black smudges on one cheek and beneath his right eye.

Xander didn't have to say anything in that moment. His appearance said it all.

The cold air rushed in behind him... or maybe it was just the way he looked that sent a chill racing down Rylee's spine, making her shiver in reaction.

"Hey," he rasped, inhaling a deep breath that made his chest swell.

"Hey," Rylee whispered, eyes darting between his, trying to read him.

His broad shoulders looked heavier. Like something was weighing them down. Something he couldn't just set aside. And only looking at him had Rylee feeling it in her chest too before he told her anything.

"*Umm...*" He cleared his throat, then ran a hand through his deep brown locs, the motion slow, like he needed something to do with his nerves. "I know you asked me to give some space between me and the kids, and I'm trying, Snoop. I am, but *uh...*"

He squeezed his eyes closed, and that was all it took for Rylee to go to him.

She pressed her hands to either side of his face, making him look at her.

He exhaled all the air he seemed to have in him, dropping his head a little in her cradling hands.

"I lost two kids in a house fire two hours ago..."

Rylee gasped.

"And I just..." Tears slid from his eyes and Rylee caught them, wiping them away. "I just *need* to be around joy right now. And I know where to find it—"

Rylee cut his words short, balancing herself on the arches of her feet to wrap her arms around him the best she could.

A short second later she stepped back and invited Xander into the brownstone.

His Jordans had yet to step off the welcome mat, when Nova and LJ shouted, "Uncle Xander!"

The two children dropped the Legos they were playing with to run up to Xander, wrapping their little arms around each of his legs.

And that smile Rylee noticed was missing on Xander had instantly returned.

"What are you guys still doing up so late?" Xander asked as he kneeled to give the children a hug.

His voice didn't sound the same in this state. It sounded broken, strained, and hearing that made Rylee's heart ache even more.

"Mommy was cleaning but then we're going to sleep," Nova informed.

"Oh!" LJ shouted. "Can you read us our bedtime story, *pleaseee*?"

Xander peeked back at Rylee, and all Rylee did was nod.

"Of course," Xander promised with a nod of his own. "I'll read you both one. How does that sound?"

"Great!" LJ expressed with a playful jump like a superhero.

Xander laughed, scooping up the children. "Aight, so let's go."

"Uncle Xander," Nova said as Xander carried the children, one on each arm, up the stairs effortlessly. "You smell a little funny... like that black stuff my Grandpa Gannon makes barbecue with."

"Yeah," Rylee heard Xander say as he reached the top of the stairs. "Uncle Xander had some kind of day."

As always, Nova and LJ didn't even look back at Rylee. They just buried themselves in Xander's embrace on the way to their rooms like he'd always been part of the blueprint that were their lives. And maybe... he had become that.

Rylee squeezed her eyes closed and shook her head, attempting to shake the thought while making her way to the living room to clean up the Legos.

Any other night, Xander popping up without calling first would have gotten under her skin, but based on Xander's mood when he arrived and based on what he said happened, he needed this. And Rylee was willing to let it go... this once.

After the Legos, Rylee made her way up to the rooms. She checked Nova's room to see she was already in bed, tucked in, and dozing off.

She could hear Xander reading the last of the few lines to LJ in his room and made her way there.

When she arrived, she watched from the doorway, as Xander read to a drowsy LJ. Xander's hulking figure, sitting in the chair Rylee kept in LJ's room for herself to sit and read to him.

Her heart was full and aching at the same time. But for once, as she watched Xander be the amazing man he's been from the start, she doesn't resist the warmth. She lets that warmth and the view of her son and her man wash over her.

She stepped back as Xander stood from his seat. He extended his fist for LJ to bump and wished him a goodnight before leaving LJ's room and shutting the door gently.

"Thanks," he said low. "As simple as that was and maybe inconvenient, I needed that, for real. I appreciate it."

Rylee watched as Xander pinched the corners of his eyes before running his hand down his face.

"I should get going." He grabbed the bottom of his jacket to zip. "Long day, and I need a shower bad." He smiled next. "Because as Nova told me, I smell funny."

Rylee smiled back, reaching for his hand and stepping closer to him.

"You don't have to go," she told him low. "Not tonight. You shouldn't be by yourself tonight."

This was one of the things that made Rylee uneasy about dating a firefighter. Though he's often assured her that a majority of the work he did as a firefighter was not dangerous or life-threatening, every so often they got a call that was.

And tonight, Xander had gotten that call.

But instead of telling him, *"See, this is what I worry about,"* Rylee chose to extend that joy he was seeking when he showed up at her brownstone.

So she walked him into her bedroom, closed the door behind them, and helped him undress in silence... not out of lust, but out of love. Then she watched him retreat to her en suite, knowing some grief had to be washed away before it could be touched.

He spent a little extra time in there, more than usual. When she'd peek inside through the gap in the en suite's door, she'd seen his hands planted against the shower wall, his head slung forward. Xander just stood there as the water poured down on him.

But she waited, the wait giving her an opportunity to realize this was the first time she'd let him stay without excuses or feeling guilt.

And that made things feel different.

She was laying in the bed when Xander emerged out of the bathroom. Rylee had decided to get comfortable when she noticed him taking longer than usual in the en suite.

Xander kept a few of his things in Rylee's room, including the boxers he pulled from the drawer in the bathroom.

All six-foot-something of him swaggered to her in bed. She almost felt embarrassed by how she was admiring his physique at a time she felt she shouldn't have been.

Instead of heading to his usual side of the bed, he peeled back her covers and climbed on top of her... not to take, but to rest.

Not in a way to initiate sex, either. He laid on top of her for comfort.

The moment Rylee spread her arms wide enough for him to bury his face against the tee she wore, it didn't take long for Xander's shoulders to shrug in the cry he tried to muffle against Rylee.

Her arms curled tighter around him, the heat of his skin bleeding through the cotton of her tee, her hand drifting slowly up and down the ridges of his back.

Two kids. He'd lost two kids and for how much Xander loved children, she knew he was really feeling the loss that night.

So she held him as tight as she would her kids whenever they hurt themselves. Allowed Xander's tears to dampen the fibers of her tee. Her fingers stroked his damp locs—neatly rolled, despite his day, and still warm from the shower—offering the comfort he didn't know he needed.

No questions, no checking if he was okay.

He would let her know everything when he was ready.

When his shoulders finally relaxed, Rylee took his face in her hands, lifting his head so she could look into his eyes.

And he let her.

Allowed her to see the red-streaked whites of them. How the puffiness of them were proof that this was not his first cry of the night.

They held their stare for a bit before Rylee tugged at him just right and lifted her head high enough to press a kiss to his lips.

With her conversation with her friends from earlier that day at brunch playing in the back of her head, Rylee let Xander in with that kiss in a way she hadn't before. That moment, in her bed, with Xander laying on her for comfort, was the first nonverbal yes she'd ever given to the idea of them without hesitation.

Xander balanced himself on his strong arms to bring himself closer to her.

She moaned at the weight of him on her, which inspired her to pull her legs from beneath him to spread them instead so he could position himself between them.

A low groan rumbled through her chest as the heat between them bloomed.

She blindly reached for the night table's drawer, opening it and grabbing a condom, sight unseen. Ripped the wrapper open mid-kiss and lowered it between them. Xander assisted, pulling himself out of his boxers so Rylee could slide the condom over his growing erection.

Xander made enough room between them to aid her actions, then raised himself higher, slid her panties to the side so he could sink his hard into her soft.

Rylee whimpered as he guided himself in slowly.

"*Mmm*," he moaned, his tongue still entangled with hers as he pulled back under the covers to push into her again.

Did that enough times to make Rylee break the kiss to get lost in the rhythmic strokes he always knew how to give... even in grief.

Xander did that for a little, removing his boxers in the act before turning Rylee over onto her stomach to remove her panties next. He guided himself in once more, this time not as slow as the first time.

Pressed his lips to her ear and filled her listening space with exhales that mirrored his thrusts, making her bury her lips into the pillow so she couldn't be heard enjoying it all.

The weight of Xander inside and over her. His presence not only in her bed but in her space.

How could something that felt so right make her feel guilty too?

And any other night, she would have let that question haunt her, as her body gradually softened to the point she could hear her heart's rhythm in her ears. Her body growing statue-still, her inner walls fluttering on their own, and her moans reduced to just heavy breaths.

"Rylee, *mmm*..." Xander breathed in her ear, shuttering his strokes now. "You feel like peace right now, baby. Just like it."

When nothing could be heard after that between them besides

her body's natural lubrication and Xander's deep dives and guttural grunts…

And when all that remained was the ringing in their ears, the pounding of hearts, and the soft clap of skin against skin, Rylee surrendered blissfully to the now—feeling as though she'd been catapulted so high that only the wrap of Xander's arms around her waist could ground her again.

He held her close and pressed breathless kisses up her shoulders and against her neck, turning her onto her back to kiss her again, making Rylee feel like she would melt into the sheets.

After a moment of catching their breaths together, Xander fell to his pillow, bringing Rylee with him. She rested her head on his chest, listening to the galloping of his heart, holding him tighter against herself.

In that position, her eyes drifted to the photo of Lennox she kept on the night table.

Unlike other times, the sight of Lennox's photo doesn't stir panic inside her. It doesn't make her flinch or feel disloyal or brace for regret.

All she felt was… acceptance.

Warm and steady as Xander's arms around her.

An acceptance that made her close her eyes and let herself be held.

*five*

RYLEE

"I GOT YOU THIS," Rylee said, opening her sparkling silver clutch and pulling out an envelope.

Xander straightened, curiosity narrowing his eyes as she slid it across the table to him.

He lifted the flap of the white envelope and smiled as he retrieved the card inside.

Rylee smiled back.

"Got you this, too," she added, pinching the silk-like string of a white organza favor bag filled with candy-coated chocolates. Rylee lifted it out of her clutch and placed it in his hand.

The second he recognized his favorite candies, Xander laughed, tossing his head back as the bag crinkled in his palm.

"I had the kids help me single out the blue ones just for you, since we know those are your favorite."

"Damn, I'm loved." He tried to suppress the tight pull of his silly grin but couldn't help but give in. "Thank you, baby."

She winked. "You're welcome. You deserve."

Night had fully settled by the time they boarded The Hudson Gem, a glass-enclosed dinner yacht departing from Manhattan's

Chelsea Piers. Seated across from each other in their best, they looked like a red carpet couple.

It was Xander's idea for them to enjoy a date night. His thank-you for the night she held him together.

The kids were home with their nanny, Abeni. Xander had promised them a day at Coney Island come spring, as his thank-you to them.

"I love you, just because..." Xander read aloud, eyes skimming the sweet paragraph handwritten by Rylee. "Just because you deserve to be reminded. Just because your presence brings peace. Just because I love you. No reason needed." He looked up at her. "*Aww*, baby."

She'd even had Nova and LJ write their own little notes on the blank side of the card, addressed to their *Uncle Xander* in their own handwriting.

Xander closed the card and pressed it to his chest, eyes shut for a brief moment. "I love this a lot."

Rylee's eyes glistened. "I love you."

The yacht had set sail about fifteen minutes earlier, so guests were still settling in. They would cruise down the Hudson River, past Lower Manhattan, around the Statue of Liberty, and back to Chelsea Piers, offering panoramic views of the city skyline.

The view through the floor-to-ceiling windows was already breathtaking. The night skyline shimmered on the water like stretched diamonds, a golden glow of city lights glinting against the dark sky. New York's version of the Emerald City.

Aside from the occasional ferry horn, soft jazz played in the background, blending with the low hum of chatter around them.

Like them, other couples sat at candlelit tables, the mood set, the vibe perfect.

"This is beautiful," Rylee said, her eyes glued to the view beyond the glass. The entire yacht was wrapped in glass, offering a 360-degree view of the city.

Rylee thought of how she and Lennox used to steal Friday nights for themselves. Rooftop dinners, tucked-away bistros, late reservations. But this... this felt like something entirely different. Something that could be just hers.

"*You're* beautiful," Xander said, pulling her attention back to the now. "So *very* beautiful."

And she was.

At his request, Rylee had dressed like the paparazzi knew her name. She'd practically had to blow the dust off her emerald satin dress. It had been a long time since she'd needed to dress up for a place that called for it. She paired it with a faux white pelted fur coat, and in her ears were her favorite nameplate bamboo *Rylee* earrings, still a favorite after all these years.

"*Mmm*," Xander moaned, his attention soft, eyes slightly hooded. "You look so good tonight, Rylee. Damn."

She giggled. Might've blushed if she could. "Thank you. And you look better than these dinner options."

He chuckled, licking his lips.

And he did. Gone were the hoodies, joggers, and tees. Xander cleaned up in a green dress shirt to match her dress—top two buttons undone—tailored slacks, and brushed leather Chelsea boots.

They both looked good. On the outside, and in spirit.

Their server arrived and took their orders, returning shortly with two glasses of white wine and a shared charcuterie plate of fig jam, prosciutto, brie, and crackers. For her appetizer, Rylee chose the shrimp cocktail. Xander went with the crab cakes.

As they reached across to sample from each other's plates, Rylee couldn't help but feel... good.

Which was necessary.

Because she knew in a few days, that would change.

Minutes into their appetizer, Xander leaned back into his plush seat, eyes on the skyline, his expression more peaceful than she'd seen in days.

She watched quietly, struck by how easily Xander could still make her heart flutter, without even trying.

"How are you feeling today?" she asked, gently dabbing her mouth with her napkin.

Xander inhaled a deep breath, his broad chest swelling beneath his green dress shirt.

"Better," he said with a nod, eyes returning to hers. "Thanks to you."

He reached for her hand. Rylee gave it to him without delay.

"You didn't just sit with me that night," he said, eyes steady on hers. "You brought me back. Because before I stopped by... *hmph*. I was feeling *really* bad, Snoop."

Rylee rubbed her thumb over the back of his hand. She'd never forget the look in his eyes when she opened the door and saw him standing there, broken, so unlike himself.

"You've done the same for me," she said softly. "So many times. Without even trying. Probably without even realizing it."

A small smile tugged at one corner of Xander's mouth. "Good. Knowing that makes me feel good."

When it was time to order dinner, Xander chose the pan-seared salmon with risotto and broccolini. Rylee ordered the lemon-garlic pasta with scallops.

"Another glass for her, please," Xander said, motioning to her nearly empty wine glass.

She considered declining—she was already feeling the buzz from the first—but tonight, she wanted to savor every moment.

In just a few days, the anniversary of Lennox's death would arrive. The upcoming Wednesday. Every year, it came like clockwork, and every year she dreaded it. Xander never knew. She never told him. So this dinner cruise, this gesture, came right on time.

For a while, they dined in easy silence, the only sounds between them were the gentle tap and scrape of silverware against their plates. Rylee tried to stay present, but a soft pang had settled in her chest.

"Where are you right now?"

His question pulled her up from her thoughts.

She looked up from her plate, blinking away the fog. His voice had been gentle, low, but still audible over the soft jazz and ambient conversation around them.

She shifted in her seat, crossing her legs beneath the table.

Rylee considered telling him the truth. That the anniversary of Lennox's death was heavy on her mind tonight. That the ache was already starting. And she hated how it sneaked up on her year after year and unraveled her without warning.

But instead, she pivoted.

"I was just thinking about how Nova and LJ have been arguing again." She lifted her glass and sipped. "LJ's back to being bothered about her room being bigger."

Xander chuckled. "You know that boy wants everything equal. Especially when it comes to his big sister."

"*Mmm-hmm,*" she agreed, shaking her head.

"That's why I'm intentional with always being fair with them." He grinned. "That boy don't play about stuff like that."

"At all," Rylee said, laughing with him.

To have someone who understood her children so well—who *loved* them enough to *know* them—wasn't just comforting. It was profound. But it stirred something else in her, too. Something heavier. A quiet guilt she couldn't shake.

"You ever think about giving him more space?" Xander asked.

Rylee's brow lifted. She froze, her smile fading.

*What did he mean?*

"You mean like... moving?" she asked, her tone edged with unintentional defensiveness.

Xander held her gaze, unfazed. He shook his head quickly. "Nah, not like that. Just... you know, whatever feels right for them. That's all I meant."

She let out a breath she didn't realize she was holding. Her shoulders softened.

"Oh. Yeah," she said, shifting in her seat. "I mean... I do. I just... I don't want to think about changing too much right now."

*Not when so much already feels like it's shifting without my permission.*

It was a thought she kept to herself. Just like she kept the truth about what was on her mind that night. Not when one of those changes—the most unexpected one—was how much her love for the man seated across from her was deepening.

A man who handled her heart with such tenderness. Who never pushed, just showed up.

Still, the guilt clung like a shadow. She could've told him. Could've confessed the truth about what was weighing on her. But she didn't.

Once their plates were cleared and dessert arrived—dark chocolate lava cake with fresh raspberries—Xander lifted the espresso shots he ordered and held his glass in the air.

Rylee raised hers and tapped it gently against his.

The soft *clink* of glass made her laugh, and her humor was breathy and unguarded.

She was going to enjoy this night.

Because when Wednesday came, her heart would ache all over again, reminding her of everything she once lost.

"Firehouse tradition," Xander said, bringing the shot to his lips. "Take it to the head, baby."

The wine, the shots, the yacht, the moment. Rylee was on a natural high. Her eyes stayed fixed on the glittering skyline as she scooped a forkful of cake, closed her eyes, and let the rich taste of chocolate melt on her tongue.

The city shimmered even more at that hour, like a dream. For a brief second, she felt suspended between worlds.

"You aight?" Xander asked, reaching for her hand and drawing her attention back to him.

And once again, light poured in... at least that's what it felt like when she redirected her focus his way.

*God, he's beautiful*, she thought.

Tats peeking through his shirt collar. Locs pulled back and

sparkling under the yacht's lights. That smooth brown gaze locked on hers like she was the only thing in his world.

How could she not be good?

She was... for the most part.

Rylee was tempted to mention Wednesday, yet again. To break the spell. But instead, she said, "I was just thinking how lucky I am to know someone like you."

He smiled. "Same, baby."

Their eyes stayed locked... soft, warm, and unhurried.

Xander brushed his thumb back and forth along her skin, saying everything she needed without speaking. The warmth in her chest bloomed, weighing her lids, sending butterflies tumbling in her stomach.

"*Mmm-hmm.*" He licked his lips, that familiar look darkening in his eyes. "I know that look *very* well."

Rylee bit her bottom lip, holding back a smile.

"The wine done hit," he added, voice low and teasing.

A laugh burst out of her, shattering every shadowed thought that had tried to sneak in.

That feeling lingered as dinner ended, as she gathered her things and stepped outside with Xander to the yacht's railing, braving the New York winter night.

Xander stood behind her, big arms wrapped around her waist, giving just the right amount of heat to keep her warm.

Rylee leaned her head back against his chest as the boat neared the dock, her gaze tracing the towering skyline.

Then he pressed a kiss to the top of her braids, and left his lips there.

"Can I say something, and you not trip?"

"Sure." Rylee smiled faintly, eyes still trained on the skyline.

"I can't help but feel you've been spacing out on me, tonight, Snoop," Xander whispered.

"I'm not." She shook her head softly. "Just enjoying the now, is all."

"You sure?" he asked gently, his voice barely above a whisper.

She didn't answer right away but the words were right there. They were always right there. For a moment, she considered telling him... about Wednesday, about the ache that never fully faded this time of year. But instead, she pressed her hand over his, squeezing lightly.

"I'm sure."

Xander brushed his lips over her braids.

"Well, whether you're here, or somewhere else in that beautiful head of yours... " He wrapped his arms tighter. "That's where I'm tryna be."

She closed her eyes in his embrace, letting herself settle deeper into his warmth, her breath syncing with his.

Rylee wanted so badly to make this feeling last. To freeze time.

Dare to dream...

If only the ache didn't always return when the dreaming stopped.

## XANDER

XANDER SIGHED as he raised his phone within sight to end the call he'd just placed. He had just called Rylee for the third time that day. Been calling her since the day before to no answer.

It was a Wednesday. Xander's day off. He'd been working two back-to-back shifts for the past two days and was looking forward to linking up with Rylee.

It was late afternoon. He fought the feeling of reaching out in the morning knowing she would be working. But with her not answering his call for the second day in a row, things were feeling a little off. Which was odd to him, since they'd just had an incredible date night, days ago.

He shifted his position on his leather sectional that was pushed up against the exposed brick wall in his apartment, getting comfortable.

He couldn't stop his mind from wandering, thinking that maybe her silence had something to do with him popping up last week after that tragic house fire his ladder company were called to.

*Nah, that can't be it*, he reasoned.

She gave him the card and the candies at dinner. She seemed a little spaced out at times that night, true. But overall... things were good.

Xander swallowed hard in that instance, recalling that house fire. Recalling breaking into one of the rooms to see the two children holed up in a closet, unconscious and already gone, but Xander being Xander... retrieving them and administering CPR like his life depended on it outside, only for nothing to work.

He wasn't to blame. But you couldn't tell him that.

Even Rylee told him that after they made love and he held her in his arms that night.

But Xander couldn't and would never accept that.

He inhaled a deep breath, shook his head, and brought his phone within eyesight again.

Any other time he would just let it be. He promised to give her space. He was sure she could see his phone calls, so if she didn't answer, it was because she didn't want to.

And that would have been fine yesterday when she didn't answer.

But her not answering today made him feel something was just... off.

Xander pushed himself up and into a seat on his couch and leaned forward, staring at his phone.

Considered sending her a text, his finger hovering over the text app, but decided against it.

Instead, he navigated to his contacts, sorted through the C's and tapped his thumb on Rylee's mother's name.

As soon as the phone started to trill, Xander was up on his feet, mindlessly pacing.

Not nervous to speak with Rylee's mother, Claudia.

Nervous about discovering what Rylee's silence was all about.

*Was she through with me? Avoiding me?*

"Hey Xander," Claudia answered on the second ring.

"Hey, Claudia," he replied with a smile, dragging his hand through his locs, the faded sides catching light. "How are you?"

"I don't know yet," she replied, giggling. "I was good until I got this call and because you don't often call me, I'm a little nervous. What's up? Is your mama okay?"

His eyes moved to the chalkboard he kept in his kitchen with white-scribbled motivational quotes on the black surface.

"Yeah, she's good. She's great," he replied quickly. "I'm actually calling about Rylee."

"Okay..."

"I apologize for bringing you into this, but I have been calling her from yesterday and she hasn't answered any of my phone calls." He ran his hand down his face. "And I'm a little worried." He held his hand up in front of him next as if she could see him. "And I'm not worried about being dumped or ghosted or anything, 'cause you know if I *am* being dumped—"

"*Oh*, Xander," Claudia sighed on the line, and that did nothing for Xander's anxiety. "I'm sure it's not any of those things, love. This time of year is tough for Rylee."

Xander stopped pacing, his attention solely on Claudia's voice.

"Yesterday was Lennox's birthday, and today marks the anniversary of when he passed away."

Xander's heart clenched before his jaw dropped.

*So that's what that was,* he thought.

His hand was at his mouth when he whispered into it, "Oh my God."

*That's why she seemed spaced out at dinner.*

"She usually cuts the world out on this day," Claudia explained. "Likes to be by herself. Process, you know?"

Xander nodded as if Claudia could see him.

"Either Gannon and I or Lennox's parents take the kids so that she can have time to herself," Claudia continued. "She *never* asks, but we just do it."

"I can't believe I didn't remember that," Xander said to himself. "For the last two years I've worked on these days or didn't really notice... *damn.*"

"It's okay, it's fine," Claudia assured. "You wouldn't know unless *she* told you. And she wouldn't have."

Xander dropped himself into a seat on his leather sectional, shaking his head. "So, like what do y'all usually do? Wait it out?"

"Yup," Claudia replied. "We wait it out. By tomorrow she'll likely reach out."

"*Hmph,*" Xander replied, his eyes scanning the wooden floors in his apartment.

After a few more minutes of talking, Xander hung up with Claudia and sat thinking in his seat.

*"Wait it out,"* she'd advised… but that didn't sit right with him.

He twisted his lips to one side, thinking, eyes moving around his space—falling on the wall-mounted TV, his record player, then the wide, winter-gray sky beyond the window.

"Nah." He shook his head, standing to his feet.

*Waiting it out* might work for Rylee's girlfriends and her parents, but for Xander, the idea of his woman feeling anything less than happy in that moment made it seem impossible for him to sit in his apartment and wait it out.

Not when the woman he loved was probably bawling her eyes out, curled up in grief, and alone without him.

If he couldn't take her pain, he'd at least bring her comfort.

So he grabbed his bubble coat, pushed his socked feet into his Timberland boots, and left his place en route to hers.

But first, he stopped at a few places to grab some of the things he noticed she liked.

Like the lemon-mint tea blend he always loved the smell of whenever she enjoyed it in her mug—which was rare, since she loved drinking coffee more than tea.

And some fresh jasmine flowers he noticed she liked to keep by her bedside.

Xander finished his errands picking up the tacos he introduced her to years ago at a food truck alley.

The food truck owners had created a fundraiser to pony up

money to rent out a brick-and-mortar location, which was where Xander now patronized to get Rylee's favorite tacos.

With everything secure in bags, he drove them to the brownstone, holding everything in hand after parking and stepping out of his truck.

At the front door, he knocked twice.

And when he didn't get an answer, he rang the bell twice too.

Rubbed his lips together when both attempts didn't get an answer.

He inhaled a deep breath when he dropped his attention to the bushes by Rylee's trash.

Xander set the things down on the stoop and jogged down the stairs to those bushes.

Stuck his hand into the rough bristles, feeling for the fake rock Rylee kept there.

After he admitted to finding the spare keys, she revealed to him that she kept the keys there after misplacing her keys at a Mommy and Me meetup at Brooklyn's Botanical Gardens.

Xander teased her about it, saying it was bold of her to do that—living in New York City, behaving like she was in Pleasantville and leaving her keys accessible for home intruders.

But in that instance, he was happy he discovered the spare, especially with her not answering his calls, his knocks, or the ringing of her bell.

Xander didn't hesitate to push the keys into the locks.

Didn't give it a second thought when he opened her door and stepped inside.

All of the lights were off in the brownstone, the air quiet and still.

Of all the years he and Rylee had been together, the house had never seemed so still, so eerie.

Its energy gave Xander goosebumps and sent a chill racing down his back, making him shiver.

He thought about calling out her name but decided against it.

Instead, he stepped out of his Timberland boots, placed the food and items down for only a moment to remove his coat, then went searching for Rylee.

He checked the living room and kitchen, of course, and when his search came up empty, he climbed the steps to her room.

Knowing the children were at her parents' home, he knew she wouldn't be in their bedrooms, so he went straight to the master bedroom.

And when he turned the doorknob, he opened the door to see Rylee curled up into a ball on the large bed.

Xander's shoulders sank instantly.

His heavy sigh made her stir in bed, and not wanting to startle her he spoke softly. "Snoop."

Rylee gasped, lifting her head then moving the covers out of her eyes to see him standing there.

"Sorry," he apologized, noticing he startled her. "I tried calling. I... *uh*... I used the key under the fake rock you keep in the bush—"

He cut his words short when he got a good look at her, because it was impossible for him to continue speaking.

She was beautiful as always, but her smile was missing.

A frown weighed her pretty lips down, but nothing could compare to her eyes.

They were sad. So very sad.

Puffy and red. And so not the Rylee he knew.

"*Aw*, baby," he whispered, blindly setting the things down on the ottoman in front of her bed.

Her face folded into absolute grief as tears seemed to start pouring instantly.

Xander went to her, sitting on the bed beside her and pulling her to him.

She cried silently against him, and he let her.

It was on this same bed only a week ago she had let him do the same.

*How could I have not known?* he wondered.

Yes, Rylee hadn't reminded him. Nor should she have felt like she needed to, according to him.

In that moment, Xander felt a pang of guilt for not knowing—or for not pushing just a little harder—for her to tell him what was really on her mind during their dinner date.

"I bought you a few things," he whispered against her braids, leaving a kiss there. "That lemon thing you like drinking sometimes. Tacos."

She said nothing. Just sniffed back the tears that hadn't fallen.

"I even got that fizzy stuff you like putting in your bath," he confirmed, a small smile pulling at his lips. "That cupcake-shaped bath bomb thingy."

Rylee said nothing in response, and all her silence did was ache his heart just a little more.

Xander felt like he had to do something—anything—so he told her, "I think you could use one of those baths right now. I'mma go run the water for you. Cool?"

There was silence and stillness at first, until Rylee gave Xander just a glimmer of hope by nodding her answer.

The moment Xander stood from his spot, Rylee was back to being a ball in bed, pulling the covers over herself.

He glanced at her for another moment, forcing himself to step into her en suite to run the bath in the solo tub beside the stall.

*How could I wait something like this out?* he asked himself.

Seeing her like that and leaving her alone just didn't seem like an option.

As soon as the water was running and at a temperature Xander felt was suitable, he dropped the bath bomb, watching it fizz and transform the bath water from clear to powder pink.

He set up the jasmine by her tub, going to her soon after.

"Aight, it's set up for you," he told her, gently moving the covers off her. "You ready?"

All she did was nod, sitting up with his help.

Xander scanned her face, sadness etched beautifully on it.

It both broke his heart and put it back together seeing her like that. He hated to see it but wanted to be there to make it right too.

So he undressed her, removing the hoodie that looked several sizes too big for her.

He was removing her leggings when he realized the hoodie was a men's hoodie.

And it didn't take long to notice it wasn't his.

It had to have belonged to Lennox.

He swallowed hard at that assumption, dismissed the thought as he walked her to the water and helped her inside.

Rylee sat back in the tub, closing her eyes.

Xander forced his attention away from how the bath bomb's suds bubbled against Rylee's full breasts, instead leaning forward to press a kiss to her forehead.

"I'm gonna set up the tacos for you, aight?"

She'd only nodded, eyes still closed.

Xander handled the setup, even left the room to get drinks.

When he returned and checked on Rylee, he noticed her bathing herself, soaping her body, and that gave him some relief.

After a little more time, he was back in the bathroom, with a towel, helping her out.

Gave her the space to do what she usually did after a bath—moisturize her skin, slip into her cotton robe.

And when she returned to her room and sat on her bed, she spoke her first words.

"I really hate this day," she admitted, right before biting into her taco.

Xander nodded. "I know."

They ate their tacos in silence, Xander watching her the whole time.

What he wouldn't have done to take the pain off her—even for a moment—so he could see the woman he loved happy again, even for just a second.

He'd much rather her chastise him for not only popping up yet again, but for waltzing into her home after using her emergency key without her permission.

Anything but this.

After they finished eating, Rylee said she wanted to lay down again. So, Xander facilitated that, clearing the containers, making her bed, and getting into it with her.

Instead of curling up into a ball like how he found her, she curled up against Xander.

Rylee buried her face in his chest and cried.

Her tears bled through his tee, making him hold her closer to himself.

He held her how she held him—but even tighter.

And he didn't stop her. Didn't speak.

Xander just held her close while stroking her back... slowly, lovingly.

Then, he told her, "You don't *ever* have to hold it in with me, Snoop. You don't ever have to do that with me."

Rylee nodded her understanding, pressing her face even firmer against him, fisting his shirt until her sobs transitioned to her just sniffing back her tears.

They laid there, Xander rubbing her back, loving the feel of her in his arms, but hating why they were in that position.

She was hurting, and there was nothing he could do about that.

And that was a fact that made him want to speed up time so she could get past this day.

The hand that fisted his shirt moved beneath it.

Xander didn't mind. It wasn't anything new.

Rylee loved running her hands up and down his stomach, her fingertips gliding along the ripples of muscles there.

But soon her soft touches turned to caresses, something Xander's body noticed before his mind could process the shift.

He lowered his attention to her hand, and it was like as soon as he paid that hand attention, Rylee stopped herself.

She was pulling her hand from under his shirt when he pressed his hand on top of hers, stopping her from moving it.

"Why'd you stop?" he asked low.

Rylee sighed, shaking her head.

He wanted to push, get her to say what he suspected. Instead, he chose to be direct for the both of them.

"You deserve to feel good, Rylee."

Xander's eyes were on her, focused on the top of her head, but kept his attention there as if he were looking into her beautiful eyes.

"And if you wanted me to make you feel good right now... I could do that."

With that, he moved his hand under his shirt, placing it against hers again.

He encouraged her to move it in the same caressing pattern she was doing before she stopped herself.

She looked up at him, her eyes red, just as puffy, probably even more than they were when Xander first arrived.

The sight alone made the corners of his eyes prick with tears.

"I'm here for you in whatever way you need me to be here for you," he reminded, eyes locked with hers. "*Whatever* way. You understand?"

Rylee's eyes darted between his for a beat, maybe two, before she slowly lifted herself from her resting position to climb up Xander— only stopping when she softly pressed a kiss to his lips.

Xander always understood that cue.

A kiss... then a twist... him on top, or taking control in some way.

But that day, he just laid there and let Rylee move at her own pace.

He kissed her back as she straddled him.

Let her dip her hand into his boxers to pull out his erection in one smooth move.

Not rehearsed. Just a routine they'd developed between them that felt lived-in.

The only difference was that instead of reaching for the night table's drawer like she usually did, she just moved the hem of her robe out of the way so she could guide him in between her wet walls.

Xander groaned the more she rested her weight on him.

It was the first time he'd felt her with nothing between them, and he bit his tongue on purpose to keep grounded in the new feeling.

He grunted in rhythm as Rylee rolled her hips, pressing her hand to his chest for leverage.

Her eyes were closed, mouth slung open, and her head tipped back, surrendering to the motion. The feeling.

He watched it all, noticing as the goosebumps graced her skin in waves, like a video of a timelapse from day to night.

"*Mmm-hmm*, take what you need, baby," he groaned beneath her moans. He held on to her waist as she pressed into him, shuddering from the sensations he could feel building, by how her walls flexed around his stiffness.

"Come here." He sat up with her, pulling her legs on either side of himself in their seated position.

She felt different to him. And no, not because there was nothing between them.

Rylee felt more open. Vulnerable.

Which made him feel more protective of her... and even more available than usual.

In his heart.

With his body.

They kept their eyes on each other, her lips parting just like her breasts, full and rising with every upward thrust he met beneath her rolling hips, framed by the fall of her open robe.

"Do I feel good, baby?"

She moaned and nodded slowly.

"Good. That's good." Xander cradled the side of her face in his hand, maintaining his rhythm, and loving how steady her eyes were on him. "You're allowed to feel this good and I'mma always make sure you do. Just let me."

Her brows relaxed into their perfect arches. Her breathing escalated.

Breasts trembling along with the rest of her frame had Xander putting more power in his upstrokes.

"I love you," she whispered.

"I love you," he returned. "Every part of you."

The moment those words left his lips...

"*Ooh*, Xander!" Rylee shouted, desperate moans following as her eyes rolled back and her head dropped forward.

Xander caught her face, lifting it to press a kiss to her, leaning her back until her back hit the mattress, and positioning himself between her thighs.

As soon as he slid back in, he lost himself.

*They* lost themselves.

In each other.

In the moment.

And after all that friction they built between them, just as Xander felt that familiar pressure rise—more than ready to pull out—Rylee tightened her thighs around him, hooking her ankles at his back, and bringing her lips to his ear.

The rush was too fierce and came so fast that Xander's words were caught in his throat.

The need to tell her he was coming and to pull out vanished... replaced with the insatiable need to go deeper. Go harder.

Rylee's moans in his ears. The suction of her walls trapping him in warmth.

She kissed his neck and ran her soft hands down his back, fueling him to keep going, leaving Xander with only one option...

To come.

His jaw dropped. Mind went blank. Body took over his actions.

His hips instinctively knew what to do as he coasted through thrusts, his release peaking.

Rylee held him close to her the whole time, making him bare his teeth as his only hope not to rocket off that bed as he pounded in then out in uncontrollable repetition.

When his frame stiffened, every bone in his body working in concert to get him to his end, Rylee pulled him down to her, crashing her lips into his... undoing him completely.

The sounds from him were unrecognizable.

So was the feeling.

Raw.

Untethered.

Absolute bliss.

Comfort like no other.

And there wasn't a damn thing he wanted to change about the moment...

Except that it ended.

Xander caught his breath against her, then, conscious of his weight on top of her, rolled off and landed on the pillow beside her.

Their routine—except this time, things were... different.

He pulled Rylee to him, and she pressed her head to his chest.

There were no words at first.

And none were necessary.

The rhythm of her heart had slowed.

The sniffling had stopped.

The moment had done its job.

And to Xander, that was all that mattered.

The room was quiet after. So quiet they could hear cars passing outside of the brownstone.

Xander's mind was everywhere but the present.

In the afterglow of fullness.

In the warmth of Rylee's skin to his skin.

"I didn't think you could be here for this part," she said in a whisper, gaining his attention again in their silence.

"I didn't think anyone could fix that feeling... make me feel something other than defeated today."

"I didn't come to fix it, baby," he told her, kissing her forehead and leaving his lips there.

"I just wanted to be here while it hurt so you weren't alone with all that."

Rylee held him tighter in that instance, saying nothing.

Again... not needing to.

A short time later, she was drifting off to sleep in his arms... leaving Xander awake, his eyes fixed on her ceiling.

And in that moment, without even thinking about it,

He decided to accept every and anything that came with loving her...

Including her undying love for another man.

*seven*

RYLEE

## "LENNY, TELL ME WHAT TO DO."

Rylee stood opposite Lennox's grave, her eyes fixed on the image of him mid-game.

The image was laser-etched into the polished black granite of his headstone. It stood tall, catching the sun that peeked through the clouds.

Fans had been to the gravesite—some as recent as earlier that week. She could tell by the fresh flowers and notes placed around the headstone.

It was something Rylee and his parents agreed should be allowed... that fan-access to the grave be permitted during certain hours of the day.

Rylee's white roses sat amongst the other flowers.

Normally, she'd sit on the custom curved bench only feet away from the headstone—the one engraved with his name and left open for those who came to visit to have a place to sit with him.

But this morning, she needed to stand.

She needed to speak with him as up close and personal as she could get.

She sighed in frustration. Ran her hand through her braids and looked off.

Her eyes fell on the sea of headstones, varying in height and width.

She squinted at the names on the headstones, many of them recognizable. This cemetery was known for being the final resting place of many who were famous in life.

Like Lennox.

"I didn't come here yesterday and I feel terrible about that," she confessed, her breath like white smoke in the air. "I feel terrible about a lot of things that happened yesterday."

That part was very true.

Xander had stopped by the brownstone.

And although Rylee had given him shit for popping up on her and her children, she was grateful for his company.

"I need you to tell me what to do," she demanded, her voice cracking, eyes watering at the fact that it would be impossible for Lennox to do what she wanted.

"Should I keep seeing Xander? Can I... keep seeing him?"

Her chest heaved as the words left her lips.

"Because..." she exhaled, her breath pluming in the air, "because I love him. And I'm only falling deeper in love with him and... the kids love him. They love him *too* much, if you ask me. And I don't want them to forget you. I don't want for them to only know that you were here and now you're not. I don't want to always get sad when I talk about you to them but happy when I talk about him..."

Her voice trailed off as she choked back a cry.

She lifted her arm to wipe at her nose with her coat's sleeve.

Rylee inhaled a deep breath and let it out through her lips.

This push and pull in her heart had been a silent battle.

On the surface, everyone couldn't help telling her how blessed she was.

To have found a man who loved her and her children with so much heart and genuineness.

But deep inside, Rylee couldn't help being so resistant... clinging to the belief that she was preserving Lennox's memory—in her heart, with their children.

To her, Lennox was irreplaceable.

But Xander... Xander was truly a gift from God.

A man who wasn't looking to fill any spots.

He was great for her, but she was having the hardest time letting him be great to her without guilt.

"I promised you I'd wait," she whispered. Said that to herself and to him.

"I *didn't* wait. And, between you and me, I feel like shit for that."

She swallowed back the cry she wanted to give into.

Not that she had the strength to cry anymore. She'd been crying for seventy-two hours straight and was exhausted.

But still... her eyes watered.

"You promised you'd always be here," she started. "That when the clouds parted and the sun came through, it was you. Well, Lenny, here I am. I *need* you right now. Talk to me."

Her bottom lip trembled as two tears streamed down her face.

"Tell me, because I need to know... is it okay?"

Rylee got down into a squat, finding it impossible to stay on her feet after the question was asked.

She knew the answer. She just really wished she could hear Lennox's voice confirming what she already knew.

"He loves Nova and LJ. *So* much. And he loves me."

She pressed her hand to her chest. "And I love him. And sometimes, when he's around, everything just feels so complete. Like, for a moment, I let myself get lost in the vibe, in the illusion that we're a *whole* family. And I forget that we're not. That they're not his but yours. And then, my heart breaks all over again."

She shook her head, then squeezed her eyes closed.

"I'm scared they'll forget you," she admitted, biting at her bottom lip.

"But I'm even more scared that they'll remember you in sadness forever because every time I mention you, I can't help but cry."

Rylee pressed her hand to his gravestone, closed her eyes, and tried to imagine his heart beating.

She could still hear it sometimes.

If she cleared her mind well enough... grounded herself in a memory of them.

What she wouldn't have given to press her ear to his chest one last time.

To listen as her heartbeat synced up with his.

Rylee sighed, her shoulders sinking a bit at the thought.

At the wish that would never be fulfilled.

"I love him, Lenny," she repeated.

"And I need to know if you're okay with that... because, you know..."

She sniffed back her tears, wiped at her face again. "If you don't want me to be with him, if you don't want him around the kids, he won't be. I won't let him. But if you do think he's perfect for us, just tell me. Send the sign. Do what you always said you'd do. Part a damn cloud. Send a light. Do something. Please!"

There was a moment of silence. Stillness.

Only the sound of the wind moving through the weeping cherry tree, barren of leaves because of the season.

Rylee refocused on the headstone, taking one final look before leaving.

"I just don't wanna get this wrong, Lenny," she said low. "Not with you. Not with our babies. So..."

She sighed, walking closer to the headstone and crouching beside it.

She pressed two fingers to her lips, then pressed them to the laser-etched image of Lennox.

"I'll be listening for you and watching for those clouds and them sun rays."

She snickered to herself, remembering how annoyed she'd be when he'd recite that line.

Her eyes knowingly moved down to the epitaph that was engraved on his headstone, word for word...

*"When the clouds part and the sun's rays rain down... that's me. Just remember to say 'what up, Lenny.'"*

It was not only a reminder for her.

It was for others who visited too. A way for Lennox to remain in memoriam for them all.

Rylee was back on her feet again, turning and walking away.

She peeked back at his headstone, a smile wanting to form, but her frown outweighed it all, weighing her lips down.

She wanted a sign... but what she didn't realize was that it had already arrived.

Quiet.

Gentle.

Growing.

She'd find out, though... sooner than she thought.

XANDER

XANDER RAISED a finger in the air to get the bartender's attention, then gestured down at his cognac for a refill.

It was loud in the bar he sat in with his friend and fellow fire-fighter, Jamal Sterling, but Xander needed the distraction of it all.

"Throwing them back kinda fast tonight, huh?" Jamal teased, smiling over the rim of his glass as he sipped the cognac he'd been nursing. "You might wanna slow down just a little."

Xander shook his head as he slid the glass closer to the approaching bartender.

"I held my woman last night as she cried over losing a man who she believes was the love of her life," Xander uttered, watching the brown liquor pour. "I should also add, said man isn't just some ordinary man. He's a fucking basketball legend. Trust me, I'm *not* throwing them back fast enough."

The bartender whistled as he twisted the bottle to avoid spilling the liquor after pouring. "This one's on the house."

Xander lifted the glass in a toast. "Good man."

The bartender saluted him as he walked off to tend to another patron.

Xander nodded toward the bartender. "That's a good man, Jay."

Jamal's humor echoed around them.

Xander and his friend Jamal had only been in the bar for all of ten minutes, and already Xander was on his third glass of cognac.

They were in a local bar not far from Xander's apartment. He was set to report for duty tomorrow and was taking his final night off to drink away the prior night.

Though he was happy to be there for Rylee, being her shoulder to cry on took a toll on him in ways he couldn't quite understand.

He ran a hand over his locs, which he'd tied back, and grunted into his glass.

Laughter and clinking glasses filled his sound space. And though the bar was just brick walls, vintage booths, and dim lighting, it was a safe haven for him in that moment.

Because last night was beyond a lot for him.

He'd already told his friend everything. It was the only reason Jamal—who Xander called Jay—left his family of four to come hang with Xander as he attempted to drown his problems in brown liquor.

The two sat in silence for a bit before a woman approached the bar on Xander's right.

He glanced at her and gave her a non-verbal greeting to be polite.

"Hey," she said with a smile.

"What's up?" he returned.

Xander was returning to sipping his drink and minding his business when the woman said, "You look like you're a regular here. What do you recommend?"

Xander smiled. "Everything, honestly."

She held his attention, refusing to break eye contact first. Instinctively, Xander's eyes lowered from hers to peek at the cleavage she kept on display through her deep V-neck sweater dress.

"Stephanie," she said, extending her hand to him. "And you are?"

Xander took her hand, which was soft in his and much smaller. "Xander."

"Xander," she repeated, her smile growing. "Beautiful name for a beautiful man."

He scoffed a laugh, looking away. Licked his lips next. "I'm getting hit on."

She giggled. "Yes, you are."

Xander chuckled this time.

This was nothing new for Xander, nor was the setting out of place for an interaction like this.

This was exactly how Xander's life used to be only three years ago. A meeting at a bar that often—if not always—led to a trip to his apartment only a block away.

And just like those past meetings, Stephanie's lingering in Xander's presence was feeling all too familiar.

"So..." She leaned in closer. "What are you getting into after you finish that drink?"

"*Hmm*," Xander expressed, lifting the cognac to sip, licking his lips then looking her way. "Going home, getting in bed, then calling my lady to tell her I love her and to wish her a good night."

"Oh." Stephanie's smile faltered a little before she fixed it back in place. "I see."

"I'm sorry," Xander apologized next.

"No, it's fine." She winked. "*Of course* you have a girl. Lucky her."

With that she walked away, and Xander watched her leave, his eyes lowering below her waist to see she had an ass to go with her ample cleavage she wasn't shy about showing.

He sucked his teeth and returned his attention to his drink.

Three years ago, he'd already be easing her out of her sweater dress by now.

Tonight, all he wanted was to, at the very least, hear Rylee's voice on the other end of his phone.

"That woman had some big ass titties and a fat ass that did absolutely nothing for me." His glass was to his lips when he mumbled, "Rylee and them kids done broke me, Jay."

Jamal hollered a laugh, slapping a hand to his friend's shoulder. "Yeah, you broken, bruh. Irreparable."

Xander couldn't help but laugh at that.

"And I don't think you wanna be saved."

"You damn right I don't wanna be saved. Shit."

He shook his head again while wrapping his big hand around the short glass.

"I'm really getting older, man." Xander chuckled to himself. "I'm out here wanting something real these days. A home. A family. A future that doesn't feel temporary. It's crazy, honestly."

"So you, like... you *really* held Rylee the whole night as she cried over dude?"

Xander sighed, closing his eyes and inhaling a deep breath. "I had to, man. It was her best friend and father of her children's death anniversary. I walked in there and saw her looking all broken, a shell of herself. I had to. So yeah, I held her as she cried in my arms and that shit led to us making love—"

"Wait, what?"

Xander blew air through his lips while squeezing his eyes closed. He lowered his head to pinch the corners of them. "I'd rather not share any more than that, Jay."

Jamal sat quietly beside Xander, not pushing for more information just yet, simply giving Xander the space.

And that was one of the reasons Jamal was his best friend, and why they'd been friends since high school, becoming firefighters together after being EMTs. Their lives were similar, except Jamal had started his family before Xander, while Xander spent more time in the bachelor life.

But things were changing for Xander in ways he never expected, and he had no desire to run from that change. He just wished falling for Rylee didn't feel like walking a tightrope with no net.

Even as the frustration tried to build when he thought about how resistant Rylee had been to him getting close to her and her kids, he remembered the night before—walking into that room and seeing her curled up in a ball. Then helping her into the tub, her eyes red-rimmed, spirit depleted... he understood the resistance. He just wished he could do something about it. Do something about the pain and her worrying about getting too close.

What did she think could go wrong?

"Holding her as she cried over him felt like the only relief I could provide," Xander shared after some silence between them. "I don't know if making love last night was right, given the circumstances or whatever, but shit…" He shook his head. "It felt like the only thing I could do to help her breathe again."

Jamal pressed his tongue to his cheek and nodded. "Was she into it?"

Xander jerked his head back then shot his friend a mean glare. "Man, Jay."

Jamal raised his hands between them. "I'm just asking."

"It wasn't like *that*," Xander insisted, fixing his eyes to Jamal. "It wasn't about the sex at all. It was the only thing I knew how to give her that didn't need words. Because words were just failing me at the time. She was crying over losing a man she loved. What the fuck can I say to that? What can I do when I love her the way she says she still loves him?"

Jamal blew air through his lips, lifting his glass of cognac to his mouth to drink. He took a moment, seeming to gather his thoughts when he asked Xander, "Are you sure she sees y'all relationship like you do? Or are you just playing husband in your head?"

Xander blinked in response.

"I just… I don't see how the hell you do it or *why* you're choosing to put yourself through this."

Xander ran his hand down his face. "I put myself through this, because… she's the love of my life and I'll do whatever the hell she needs, man. Even if it's uncomfortable sometimes. And scary—"

"Scary?" Jamal questioned.

Xander swallowed hard while shaking his head, gathering his thoughts.

"Jay, I can walk into burning buildings without blinking. You know that." Xander stared into his drink. "But the thought of Rylee deciding she doesn't want me because she can't get over the loss of her children's father?" He exhaled. "Yes. *That* shit is scary as fuck. And it's the one thing I don't know how to survive."

"Damn." Jamal slapped Xander on the shoulder again and held Xander's shoulder blade in his tight grip. "You'd be lucky to be only down bad, man."

Xander chuckled, lifting his glass to continue sipping his drink. "Tell me about it."

* * *

"OMG!" Nova shouted from the living room. "What's *that*?!"

Xander's heart melted the moment he noticed the gleam in Nova's eyes. They were focused on the bags Xander had walked into the brownstone holding. Which was a huge contrast to the look in Rylee's eyes when she opened the door to see him standing on the other side holding the bags.

"They're for you two," Xander informed, stepping out of his sneakers and walking the bags into the living room.

He didn't pop up this time. As promised, he texted Rylee to see if it would be fine for him to stop by the brownstone after his shift that evening, and she told him sure.

"I was at work on the field when we got a call to a toy store," Xander explained, setting the bags down and crouching to the kids' height. "The space was *packed* with toys."

LJ's face lit up. "From the floors to the ceiling?"

Xander smiled. "To the windows to the walls, my guy."

Rylee snorted behind him.

"Cool!" Nova chimed in.

"So, when I saw *this*," Xander remarked, pulling out the mini dollhouse. "And *this*," he added, lifting the Bill Nye virtual reality science kit from the second bag next. "I just *had* to get them for you two."

"Oh. My. God!" LJ whispered. His little jaw dropped as he picked up the kit, his eyes locked on the VR goggles. "This is *so* cool."

"Thank you, Uncle Xander!" Nova said, wrapping her little arms around Xander's neck from behind. "It's my favorite."

"Yeah!" LJ echoed next, running up to Xander and embracing him in just as tight of a hug as his big sister. "It's my favorite in the whole wide world too. Thank you."

Xander laughed as he hugged them back.

In that moment, he felt so damn full and couldn't deny it.

He hadn't planned on it. But after answering a call at a toy store —just some overheated batteries in a display—he saw the dollhouse and the science kit, and he couldn't not get them.

*"Mmm-hmm," his best friend Jamal teased, smiling at Xander as Xander paid for the toys at the register. "He lost in the sauce."*

Xander didn't mind it or care when his fellow firefighters teased him on the way back to the firehouse. They laughed and talked shit at Xander and his big self cradling bags of toys in his seat on the truck. But he didn't care. He just blocked them out, choosing to imagine the kids' reaction when he brought the toys to them. He knew it would be worth it.

And it was.

He peeked back at Rylee to see her arms folded. The moment she saw him looking at her, he noticed her force a smile. Knew it was forced by how tight it looked on her lips.

Xander arched a brow at that.

"Can we play with them, Mommy?" Nova asked. "Please, please, please!"

"Yeah," LJ chimed in. "Please!"

"Only for a little." Rylee smiled, Xander admiring the dimples adorning her cheeks. This time her smile reached her eyes. "But then you have to get ready for bed."

They all hung out in the living room for the next hour. Xander on the couch with Rylee, and the kids on the living room floor, distracted with their new toys.

"Everything good?" Xander asked, his arm draped over her shoulder.

"*Mmm-hmm,*" she replied with a nod.

He tightened his hold on her shoulder, brought her in closer so he could whisper in her ear.

"So why does it feel like you're mad at me?"

Rylee tilted her head back to look at him. Leaned in a second later to press a kiss to his lips.

"We'll talk about it after the kids go to sleep."

The smile that was on his face slowly released.

*Talk about what, exactly?* he thought to himself.

Xander was confused. Really confused... and justifiably so.

He was quiet for the next few minutes. Quiet as Rylee got up to help the kids put their toys away so they could get ready for bed. Quiet after walking with them and Rylee up the stairs, telling them goodnight from their bedroom doors, choosing to wait for Rylee out in the hall to walk with her to her bedroom.

And when they got inside her master bedroom and she closed the door, Xander got right to it.

"So?" he asked, pushing his hands into his jeans pockets.

She folded her arms. "So?"

He shrugged. "What did I do now?"

She sighed. "Xander, don't say it like that."

"Say it like what?"

"Like... *that.*" She gestured at him.

He laughed, shaking his head. "Aight, so how should I say it?"

Rylee twisted her lips to one side.

"Because I didn't pop up this time, right?"

"You didn't."

"I texted and you said it would be cool, right?"

"You did and *I* did," she replied. "But what you didn't tell me was that you were going to bring gifts."

"Oh, my God." Xander gasped exaggeratedly, then pressed a hand to his chest. "Criminal. I'm a criminal."

Rylee sucked her teeth.

"To bring gifts to the children... gifts that they loved, no less. My God." He shook his head while waving his hand in the air. "Nah, baby, you gotta call the cops on this one. Because this right here was totally reprehensible."

"Xander, please be serious."

"I *am*, call 'em!"

Rylee rolled her eyes and tried to swallow back her laugh but failed.

"You keep making them love you more."

"Disgraceful," Xander whispered, pressing his hands to either side of his face. "Shame on me. My offense just keeps getting worse and worse by the minute."

She punched him on the arm and he snorted.

"You know who's really to blame here, right?" He wagged a finger at her. "It's that Nova and her excitement. Nah, nah... it's LJ and his hugs. Them kids are trouble, Snoop. *Children of the Corn* level trouble. I'm telling you. Look what they're doing right now, getting me in trouble. Went to sleep and shit, leaving me to fend for myself in the wild. Just evil, baby."

Rylee balled her lips to keep from smiling.

"Because when I answered a call to check out a toy store and their fire alarm," he recalled, closing the distance between them and only stopping when he was close enough to wrap his arms around her waist. "And I saw those toys, I just couldn't get out of my head how happy they would be if I brought them to them. And I didn't tell you because I wanted it to be a surprise. Because yes, I love them kids..." He tilted her head back so she'd look at him. "I *really* love you. And baby, while I get your hesitation, I'm tired of getting into fist-fights with your fears. They hit *really* hard for real. And they're impossible to duck."

She scoffed a laugh.

"They giving me black eyes and busted lips and shit."

She playfully slapped his chest. "Be serious."

"I *am*, baby, see…" Xander pointed at his eye. "They got me good right here." He took her hand and pressed it to his chest against his heart. "And here."

Rylee's smile relaxed on her lips as she maintained eye contact.

There was silence between them. With the children in bed, the house was quiet on the other end of Rylee's door, allowing Xander's words to settle between them.

"I get it," Xander continued, nodding now, lifting her hand to kiss and place it by her side. "I may have thought it once before, but that day I showed up to see you so…" He swallowed hard. "So down on the anniversary of Lennox's death… I got it that day. Lennox wasn't just your friend. He wasn't just your kids' father. He was the love of your life."

He noticed when Rylee held her breath and didn't let it go. So he held her firmer against him so she would exhale what she was holding in.

"I understand that now." He nodded. "But I need you to understand this… you're mine, Rylee. You're the love of *my* life."

Her jaw slacked a little, eyes never wavering.

Xander lifted his hand to brush the side of her face with his fingers.

"I love you with everything in me." He bobbed his head up then down. "And with that, I know I have to love every part of you, including the loss and the pain. So I get it, aight?"

Her chest was rising and falling harder now.

"I need you to also know that you stole my heart and I don't want it back from you. *And…*" His arms grew firmer around her waist. "As much as you try to fight it, I know you feel the same. I can feel it every time I'm with you. Around you. I can feel it deep down in my bones. I *know* I have your heart too… what's left of it at least."

He noticed when her eyes began to water as she held their stare.

"Xander—"

Him pressing his thumb to her mouth stopped her. Xander ran

his thumb down her lips, watching as her eyes closed, then he leaned in for a kiss.

He exhaled on her lips, loving the weight of her in his arms. Parted her lips slowly to slide his tongue into her mouth in search of hers.

She moaned, like she always did. Moaned in a way that made him feel like she wasn't thinking of anything else but the two of them, there, in her bedroom.

Rylee kissed him back, her arms raising to coil around the back of his neck to take their kiss deeper.

Neither of them were in a rush. And that was clear from the kiss that was soft but aching, and filled with all the unspoken truths between them.

Xander confessed that she was the love of his life, but he didn't tell her that he laid in bed at night wishing he could be in hers instead. How he wanted so bad to go to sleep and wake up to her every night and be whatever she needed in whatever way she needed him.

He didn't say any of those things, but his kiss did. And he was sure she could feel that.

"I got a gift for you too," he said on her lips when they could break long enough for air.

Rylee smiled on his lips. "Oh?"

"*Mmm-hmm*," he answered, walking her back against her dresser. "Can I give it to you?"

Rylee grinned, her eyes locking with his. "Of course."

Xander grabbed his shirt by the back and lifted it up and over his head.

Rylee pressed her hand to his broad chest as always, caressing his tatted skin, her eyes locked with his. He loved watching her switch modes with no issues. Going from mama to this... a woman with so much fire in her eyes she could burn him right where he stood and he'd love every lick of that flame.

Xander walked between her thighs, his fingers immediately

sliding into the waistband of her leggings. He pulled them down and lowered between her legs, pulling her closer to the edge.

He wasted no time, pressing kisses to the seat of her panties, then gently moving them to the side to swipe his tongue up her slit.

Rylee's head rolled back as she rested the heels of her feet against his shoulders, getting lost on his tongue.

Xander hardened at the sounds of Rylee enjoying him. Damn near came in his jeans at the sound of her trying to silence her moans through tight lips.

He moaned with her as if he could feel what she felt. Especially when she met the tide of her orgasm with a shuddering body. She lifted her hips and circled them with his tongue that orbited her clit, then tensed up as her mouth dropped open in a silent cry.

Off the dresser and onto the bed he took her, sliding her night table's drawer open to retrieve a condom.

They hadn't spoken about the night they went without protection, and Xander believed they likely never would. They were in a relationship. Sex without protection would have eventually happened... although he didn't think it would.

As guarded as Rylee was, as protective of her little family she insisted on being, Xander thought she'd always be the careful one.

None of that mattered though after Xander got rid of the rest of her clothes and his. Erection sheathed and gliding into warmth ditched any wandering thoughts of anything tied to that night he and Rylee slept with each other to ease her pain.

Tonight, all was well between them.

He told her he loved her. Told her he wasn't going anywhere. Promised to love her just as she was... pain and all.

With each thrust forward, Rylee's walls sucked him further in, engulfing him in heat he didn't want to be free of. He prayed he'd never have to go without it... or her.

He kissed her while stroking to a silent rhythm, feeling when it got too good for her to kiss him back.

Her head would fall to the side when he elevated the pace, and he'd guide her mouth back in place against his every time.

The friction mixed with their sounds of pleasure reached a level of silence with their bodies doing most of the communicating after a while.

Xander watched as she bit down on her bottom lip, her body statue-still but moving with him, under his control. He couldn't help feeling privileged in that moment.

"I love it here," he told her, voice low and sure, stroking with his words. "Not just being inside of you like this... I love being *with* you. Period. You don't have to choose, baby. I'm here. I love you. And I'm staying."

Her eyes softened.

"I just wanna love you where you need it the most."

Silence. Then breath.

All the signs that she heard him.

He licked his lips as he slid his hand up against the mattress to provide leverage to push her legs back.

"Oh!" she moaned before tucking her lips into her mouth.

"Can you let me do that, baby?" Xander slid deeper, pushing her legs further back. "Can you?"

She nodded slowly, her hand snaking to his backside to guide him in deeper.

"That's it, baby," he whispered inches from her lips. "Bring me in. Just like that."

Her lids fluttered, head tilting back, exposing her neck, as only the whites of her eyes became visible.

Xander grunted at the sight, slowed his pace to a generous glide to make it last.

"Oh, God," her voice trembled. "*Mmm*, Xander."

His hard exhales matched his strokes until he was closing his eyes to the rush that swept through him, too, challenging his restraint and forcing him to gradually move faster to ride the wave of his release.

He felt as she clung to him, shook when he reached the peak of it all. And even though he would always try to be mindful of the crash, his arms, like always, gave out, causing him to collapse on his woman.

As always she caught him, wrapping her arms around him and holding him close. Giving him all the reasons to believe that she got him. Despite it all, she had him, and for Xander that was all that mattered.

He rolled off and onto his pillow, catching his breath but pulling her to him too.

His chest rose and fell, fighting gravity to pull in more air but blissfully struggling.

*Why couldn't I have this every night?* he wondered to himself, but still allowed himself to enjoy the moment with that question on his mind.

It was quiet in the room after that. And he couldn't tell if Rylee was still awake or if she'd fallen asleep like she usually did after they made love.

Still, Xander said to the air, "I love you, Rylee, and I don't just say that because it sounds good. I say it because I mean that."

Rylee didn't say any words back. But her tightening her grip around his waist let him know he had her attention. So he continued.

"And I love those kids. *A lot.*" He nodded. "I'm not him, baby... I know I'm not Lennox. But I swear I'll never stop showing up for you the way he would've wanted someone to. At least what I'd think he'd want if he loved you as much as I love you."

And though she didn't speak any words after that, the fact that she kept him in her hug, her head on his chest, her heart beating against his rib, for Xander... that was enough confirmation, and it would have to do.

## RYLEE

RYLEE CLIMBED THE STAIRS, headed to her bedroom, eyes down on her phone. She was scrolling through her stocks app, checking market data like stock quotes, charts, and other financial metrics.

Though parenthood had become a priority for Rylee—a stark contrast to the stockbroker she once was, stalking the floors of the New York Stock Exchange—she was still ambitious. Only now, she ran her own firm from her basement, with fewer clients and a more balanced schedule.

After putting her children to bed an hour prior, Rylee spent some time in her basement office, analyzing numbers, reading articles, as she dried her family's clothes in the dryer.

Now that the laundry was done and tucked into the basket, she carried up the stairs with one arm, Rylee used her free hand to check the stock numbers on her phone one last time before bed.

She'd stopped by the children's rooms on the way to hers. They were sound asleep and soon she would be too.

But first, she needed to fold laundry.

In her room, with the clothes piled high on her king mattress, Rylee stood over them, folding the garments neatly, her eyes bouncing from the TV—that was on a 24-hour news channel—to a pair of tiny jeans in her hands that belonged to Nova.

She'd only turned the TV on to see the weather for tomorrow so she could plan the kids' outfits accordingly for school.

It was Monday night, quiet on this side of Brooklyn, just after 10 p.m. All was well until…

"We have some breaking news out in Brooklyn tonight that is developing," the news anchor said from Rylee's TV screen. "Our reporter Candace Anthony is on the scene. Candace, can you tell us and the viewers what's happening?"

Rylee looked up from Nova's jeans to the mounted flatscreen.

"Yes, James," the reporter Candace replied. "We're coming to you live from Park Slope, Brooklyn, where an evening blaze has devastated a full commercial strip on 7th Avenue between 10th and 11th Streets."

Rylee's eyes were locked on screen.

"The three-alarm fire broke out just after six this evening, engulfing over six small businesses, including a beloved bakery, a barbershop, and a family-owned bookstore."

The scene on screen looked catastrophic. Flames still blazed behind the reporter along with plumes of black smoke rising toward the dark sky. It looked bad.

"Tragically, officials have confirmed that three firefighters have lost their lives in the line of duty."

Rylee gasped and held onto her breath.

Her mind began racing.

Park Slope. Dead firefighters.

And suddenly she remembered…

*Xander's fire company is in Park Slope.*

She walked away from the bed and approached her night table, snatching up her phone.

"Their identities have not yet been released, pending family notification."

Rylee swallowed hard as she tried to key in her phone's code fast enough to unlock it but kept getting it wrong.

It was then she realized her hands were shaking.

"Several other firefighters from Ladder Company 212 were injured, including two civilians who were treated on the scene for smoke inhalation."

"Come on," Rylee whispered when she tried again, but this time her phone remained locked, displaying the notification informing she had to wait one minute before trying again.

She sighed, then swallowed back the lump forming in her throat.

"The cause of the fire is currently under investigation, though officials suspect it may have originated from faulty electrical wiring in one of the restaurant kitchens."

Rylee's bottom lip started trembling without her control. Her mind raced with everything it shouldn't.

*What if that was Xander's fire company who was called to the scene of that fire?*

*What if Xander had been hurt?*

"Tonight, the city mourns its fallen heroes, and this Brooklyn neighborhood grapples with the sudden loss of both lives and livelihoods," Candace added, the mic to her mouth, her news station's logo emblazoned beneath the microphone's head. "I'm Candace Anthony reporting live here in Park Slope, Brooklyn. Back to you in the studio, James."

The minute felt more like an hour to Rylee, not aiding in her panic. She could hear her heart in her ears when she finally was able to try again to unlock her phone.

This time she got it open, and didn't hesitate to make her way to the phone app. She clicked in, then clicked Xander's name that appeared as one of her recent calls in her call log.

The moment she pressed the phone to her ear, she realized his phone had gone straight to voicemail.

Her heart immediately dropped.

"Oh, my God," she whispered to herself.

Her throat went dry. Legs so weak she needed to take a seat on her bed.

She tried again. Still voicemail. And again... no answer.

Rylee tried to take a moment to collect herself, tossing her phone onto the bed.

In that moment, in her panic, she tried to rack her brain to remember Xander's ladder company. He had it tatted on his arm but in that moment her brain couldn't process anything or remember that simple detail.

Her phone was in her hand again when she tried calling once more.

But again his phone went to voicemail.

She clicked out, moved to her text app. Clicked on his name and immediately went to typing.

> Rylee: Please tell me you're okay.

> Rylee: Xander??

> Rylee: Where are you???

With each moment that passed where she had no confirmation, she felt every ounce of her weight on her bones.

Her leg was bouncing in her seat on the bed, body strumming from the rush of blood that was moving throughout her too fast.

She was now shaking all over. Pressing his name over and over again in her call log only for voicemail to pick up.

"Oh, God," she cried, touching her face and realizing it was wet with tears.

*This can't be happening,* she thought to herself. *Not again. Not like this.*

She had thought she'd moved past the sharp edges of that night... the night she lost her best friend, the father of her children. But now, with no word from Xander, the grief ripped itself from the corner she'd tucked it into, reminding her it had always been there, quietly waiting to reemerge at the least opportune time.

Like now.

And just like that, she was back in Brooklyn Bay Medical Center... the night Lennox never woke up.

But the night she recalled, that was sitting as heavy on her chest as that moment with her sitting on her bed, was when her best friend Lennox was taken there.

She recalled feeling a little optimistic, because Lennox was in her father's hospital. And Lennox had passed out before but he turned out to be okay, able to walk out of the hospital once, so of course he would have to do it again.

But that night was not like the other. And Lennox never woke up.

Rylee watched her best friend take his last breath against her, watched the life leave him in front of her.

She played that moment over and over in her head so much she could remember everything about it. From the sound of his last exhale to the warmth that seemed to leave his skin as she held his hand for too long after.

Rylee squeezed her eyes closed, feeling herself sinking. She felt powerless, untethered, and unable to breathe. So she did the only thing she could think to do, the only thing she ever felt brought her relief in her moments of despair whenever thoughts of Lennox grabbed a hold of her and refused to let go.

She prayed.

Loudly.

"God *please* don't do this," she pleaded, pressing her palms tightly together and pressing her fingertips to her lips. "I know I don't talk to you often and I know I only talk to you to ask you for things but please. I am begging you to please don't take someone else I love. *Please*."

As soon as the words left her lips a cry soon followed. She got down on her bedroom's floor of her room and sobbed, doing her best to keep the sound down but finding it so hard to.

A second later, her phone rang.

She gasped, popping her head up, raising her hand to her mattress and feeling for her phone before she could balance herself on her shaky knees to look.

Xander's name appeared on the screen.

"Xander?" she exhaled into the phone. Her voice was a mix of panic and sadness, too many emotions all at once.

"Rylee?" Xander answered. "Baby, why you sound like that? What's the matter?"

Another cry left her as she asked, "Where the hell have you been?"

"Hey, hey," Xander said, his voice so calm and soothing at the same time. "What's the matter, baby?"

"I thought…" she started, finding it hard to find the words though. "There was a fire… your phone kept going straight to voicemail—"

"Aye, yo, Paulie," she heard Xander say in the background. "I'mma be right back. Handle the front for me."

There was some shuffling on Xander's end before he revealed, "My battery died. Just got it back because it was charging while I was at the front desk. I'm on my shift at the station."

"There was a fire in Park Slope," she stated, her voice shaking. "I thought—"

"Yeah, that was another fire company, baby," he cut in. "They got there before we even got the call. I'm okay. We're okay."

"I thought you were one of them," she whispered, pressing her back to her bed on the floor. Rylee sniffed back her tears, her eyes burning now.

"One of who?"

"The firefighters they said died," she answered, tears streaming down her face, her voice hoarse now, strained. "And I just… I couldn't live through that again. And I thought I'd have to."

There was silence on his end for a couple of beats.

"You don't," he said after the pause. "I'm right here, aight? And I'm on my way to you. I'll see you within the hour. Okay?"

Before Rylee could say anything else, Xander ended the call.

She cleaned her face with her hands. Her body still trembling uncontrollably as she sniffed back tears that kept falling.

Rylee stayed on her bedroom floor until she heard her doorbell downstairs. And when she took the stairs down to answer it, Xander stood on the other side.

She searched his face for burns, bandages... anything. But all she saw was him. Whole.

He had on no coat, just his station's uniform. A blue tee tucked into pressed slacks, and black boots on his feet.

She was so distraught she couldn't enjoy the view of her man in his uniform, fulfilling fantasies she didn't even know she had.

He didn't have to say a thing. Rylee closed the space between them and threw her arms around him, pressing her face into his chest and crying against him.

In that moment, she hated herself for all those times she made a fuss over him popping up without calling. Surprising her kids with gifts or promises of homemade breakfast with pancakes shaped in whatever shape they wanted.

She cried against Xander and he let her. He walked her back inside and away from the doorway, allowing her to cry into him as he closed the door, not once letting her go.

In the middle of hating herself over his pop-ups, she hated herself for doing what she did with Lennox... taking Xander for granted. Just like Lennox died suddenly, Xander could have been in that fire tonight and died too, without warning.

She vowed she would never take time for granted after Lennox, but was kind of doing it with Xander. And that made her hug him even tighter.

"Don't *ever* do that to me again," she uttered against him.

He chuckled softly, tightening his arms around her. "Do what, Snoop?"

"Not answer your phone." She sniffed back her tears and stepped back. "Because I swear—"

"My phone lost charge, baby—"

"Then keep a charger strapped to your back, Xander!"

"*Shh*," he shushed, taking her hand, his eyes moving up the stairs. "Don't wake the kids now."

"I thought..." she said, her shoulders slouching a little. "I thought I'd lost you tonight."

Xander closed the space between them again, wrapping his arms around her when he was close. He tilted her head back so she'd look up at him, then brushed his thumb under her eyes.

"You really thought I was in that fire, huh?"

"*Yes*," she exhaled, closing her eyes and nodding her head, feeling the tears pool again. "And I swear the thought of losing you had me damn near dying on my bedroom floor."

He kissed his teeth as he stepped even closer to her, bending his legs at the knees to press his forehead to hers.

"You're not gonna lose me, aight? I'm here, baby, okay? Aight?"

Rylee sniffled as she nodded against him, her hands pressing to either side of his face. To have him here, in her space, promising her something that sounded good but that she knew could change at any time, still was reassuring.

"Your job is dangerous," she whispered. "And though I knew that already, I didn't really *know* what it felt like to actually live it until tonight."

"It's not dangerous like *that*," he explained to her. "Rarely. Most days it's '*help me with my cat*'," he said in a high-pitched voice that brought a smile to Rylee's lips. "Or '*my kid locked himself in the base-ment*' kind of calls."

"*Hmph*," Rylee huffed, moving in closer to wrap her arms around him. She wanted to hold him and not let him go, not even for a second.

"I don't want you worrying too much about that though."

"I don't think that's gonna stop," she said against him, burying her face in his shirt and inhaling his natural scent. In that moment, she felt so lucky to be able to do that. She knew there was a wife or girlfriend in Brooklyn tonight who wouldn't be so privileged.

He kissed the top of her head. "Maybe not, but you know... since I'm here now, what you wanna do with me?"

She pinched him and stepped back, and that made him laugh softly.

"Do you see my face right now? Do I *look* like someone who's in the mood for any of *that* tonight?"

Xander grinned down at her. "If you give me five minutes... I can fix that."

She scoffed a laugh while shaking her head, smiling now. Relieved again.

Xander pulled her to him and kissed her forehead, leaving his lips there.

"It's me and you. I'm not going anywhere. Promise."

Rylee sighed against him, resting her weight on his chest, finally letting herself believe what he was saying. Because it sounded good and she needed to hear good things after experiencing a rush of old memories and the fear of new ones.

"I gotta head back," he told her. "I'm on call and gotta be at the station tonight. But tomorrow, when I leave, I'll come straight here, if that's okay?"

She nodded against him. "It's more than okay."

"I love you," he told her, pressing another kiss to the top of her head.

Rylee smiled and hugged him tight, pressing a kiss to his chest before leaning her head back so he could kiss her lips. And on them she replied, "I love you too."

*Oh, God,* she thought to herself as she hugged him just a little tighter than before.

This time, she wasn't begging God. She was giving thanks.

For the first time, she was so grateful to say that.

And honestly, this moment, this night, was right on time... because it marked the calm before the storm.

RYLEE

RYLEE TURNED off her side and onto her back the moment her eyes opened. It was the sanitation truck outside of her brownstone that woke her. That, and the queasiness of her stomach.

She groaned as she pulled herself up into a seated position.

Rylee shouldn't have been sleeping at that hour. It was 10 a.m., and on any other Tuesday, she would have been down in the basement in her home office, speaking with clients after dropping her children off at school.

But the kids had spent the night at Lennox's parents's home at their insistence, so they'd taken the children to school. And that was a good thing, considering how upset Rylee's stomach felt that morning.

She kicked the covers off herself and stepped off the bed, heading straight to the bathroom.

On her way there, she tried to recall what she ate the night before.

Tomato soup and a grilled cheese sandwich. She always kept it simple when it was just her and when the kids were away.

But that didn't explain it. She had a light meal that she's

prepared plenty of times in the past. It just didn't make sense how upset her stomach felt.

"Let me just brush my teeth," she reasoned with herself, as if trying to self-soothe. It was her attempt at pushing away the sensation that was creeping up her throat.

She was on the final few seconds of her brushing routine when she noted the day.

Specifically, the date.

Rylee's period was like clockwork after having her son. Though it was once irregular, now it arrived the same time every month.

But it had been a few weeks since her cycle should've started.

The realization almost made her swallow the toothpaste in her mouth.

What started as a gradual thought turned into a slow, dawning dread that crept into her mental space and held her by the throat.

"No," she whispered to herself in a tone that suggested she was being ridiculous. Rylee shook her head for effect. "No. Impossible."

Except, it wasn't.

She grabbed her phone that lay nearby to check her digital calendar. Because to her, she had to have the dates mixed up.

That's when she noticed the reminder she'd set to meet up with Xander in the next hour.

They planned to visit an Italian restaurant out in Long Island for lunch, which didn't help with her panic in that instance.

Things had been good between them. So good.

After that night a few weeks ago, when Rylee thought Xander and his fire company had been called to that fire in Park Slope, she'd been intentionally open. Less guarded. More accepting of Xander making a place for himself in her and her children's lives.

But now *this*?

She swallowed hard when the urge to gag came over her. But swallowing just made her gag harder. Before she could process what was happening, she felt last night's dinner rush up her throat, forcing her to turn on her heels and drop into a squat in front of the toilet bowl.

Sloshing sounds echoed around the en suite as Rylee heaved and coughed into the toilet.

Once her stomach felt empty again, she dropped back on her haunches and stared at the contents floating in the toilet water before flushing.

"No fucking way," she exclaimed low, closing her eyes and pressing her hands to her face.

It wasn't long before she was back on her feet, rinsing her mouth and brushing her teeth again, then heading for her closet to throw on whatever her eyes fell on so she could leave the house.

There was no way she could ignore how she was feeling. And what she'd just done.

She'd thrown up.

Rylee doesn't throw up.

The last time she threw up was when she discovered she was pregnant with LJ.

And that thought alone had her taking large steps up Brooklyn Heights' city blocks, headed straight for the pharmacy.

"Good morning," the clerk greeted the moment Rylee stepped inside.

"Good morning," Rylee forced a smile. "Can you please tell me where your pregnancy tests are?"

The question alone had her head spinning. Never did she think she'd ever need one of those things again.

And still, at the guidance of the clerk, Rylee found the test of her choosing, walked it to the register, and left with the test and a prayer that it would give her the result she was hoping for.

Negative.

She wanted the test to be negative. Needed it to be negative, actually.

Back home, in the downstairs bathroom near the brownstone's

front door, an impatient Rylee tore open the packaging, peed on the test strip, then placed it on the counter after covering it.

She didn't move an inch.

Rylee stood over the vanity, eyes fixed on the strip as her urine moved along it, the test immediately producing two pink lines.

Her gasp was slow. Loud. Nerving.

She closed her eyes and held them tight as if she were trying to erase what she saw.

There was no way it would give a result so fast.

Except, it did.

And the result confirmed she was pregnant.

"Oh, my God," she whispered. "Oh, my God, oh, my God, oh, my God…"

She had no problem figuring out how something like this could've happened.

The anniversary of Lennox's death.

It was the only time she'd had the audacity to guide Xander inside of her without a condom.

She released a long, heavy breath that sagged her shoulders and forced her to take a seat on the toilet lid beside the vanity.

*It was one time.*

At least that's what she reasoned. She'd been caught up in the moment but still aware of what she was doing. But Rylee honestly didn't think this would happen. What were the chances, honestly?

Her head was in her hands a second later, fingers running through her braids, tossing them over her shoulder before she pushed herself back to her feet.

She had to see the test again. By now, surely it had been enough time to prove she was trippin'.

Rylee believed she just had to be trippin'.

Her eyes met the test window again and just like the first time, her heart and stomach dropped.

The lines were abundantly clearer now. Two bright pink lines.

"Fuck," she whispered to herself, her voice shaky. "This can't be real life."

She and Xander had just gotten to good. She'd just started to feel okay about them.

Now this?

The test sat on the counter where she'd placed it, bright and impossible to ignore.

Rylee pressed both hands to her cheeks, trying to feel something other than panic.

She'd done this before. Stared down at proof that her life was about to change. Always alone. Always the first to know.

But before, the news was always joyfully tethered to Lennox.

With Nova, she'd told him in person.

With LJ, she'd told him in spirit.

But this time, upon discovering she was pregnant, it wasn't joy she felt first.

Fear came first.

Fear of doing it alone.

Fear of what people would think.

Fear of how much more room she'd have to make in a life that already felt full and fragile.

Underneath all of that, annoyingly steady, was something else. Something familiar.

A small, stubborn warmth.

She'd barely wrapped her mind around it and already a corner of her heart was reaching for this baby she wasn't even sure she wanted to keep.

She wasn't supposed to be here again. Not like this. Not without Lennox.

And yet, still...

Beneath the fear was something small and warm and terrifyingly hopeful.

A whisper she wasn't ready to name.

Not that she had a chance to.

The chime of her doorbell echoed around the brownstone, pulling her eyes away from the pregnancy test and toward the front door.

Rylee pulled her phone from her back pocket and saw it was already 11 a.m... the time Xander told her he'd arrive to pick her up so they could go out to lunch.

Rylee wasn't supposed to still be in bed at 10 a.m. She was supposed to have already been up. Just like she was supposed to have used a condom with Xander that night.

"Shit," she spat, debating for a moment whether to clear the pregnancy test and its packaging or not.

Not wanting to look suspicious or keep Xander waiting outside for too long, Rylee decided to just close the bathroom door.

She ran her sweaty hands down her jeans and made her way to the front door, pulling it open to find a smiling Xander on the other side.

He held up a small bag with the logo of the candle store Rylee loved to frequent in the city.

"Guess what I got?" he said, his smile growing as he winked. "Went out there this morning so we'd have something good to come back here to. I'm thinking a bath with this burning, since you like keeping your candles in the bathroom."

He laughed as he leaned in to give her a peck on the lips.

Rylee's head was somewhere between the bathroom and the front door.

The thing every woman would normally love, an on-time man, did nothing to ease her anxiety in that moment.

She was pregnant.

Rylee was so dazed and disoriented that Xander noticed it the second he leaned out of the kiss.

He tilted his head to one side. "What's that face?"

Rylee parted her lips to speak, but nothing came out.

"Oh, no. *Uh-uh*," Xander teased, stepping over the threshold and gently moving her to the side. "You not gon' look at me like I popped up without calling when you *knew* I was coming."

Rylee's heart was pounding, the words right there at the tip of her tongue... but she refused to let them fall.

"I texted," he continued, toeing off his Jordans. "And I'm on time. Not early or late, because you said no surprises."

Xander turned to look her way, then bent his knees like he always did when talking to her. "So what's up? What's this face?"

"I... I don't have a face," she insisted, forcing a smile.

He snorted. "You don't have a face, huh?"

Rylee swallowed hard.

"You definitely got a face, Snoop."

Xander stood to his full height and lifted her chin to give her another peck on the lips. This one deeper.

"A very beautiful face."

She sighed, blowing the air out through her lips after he stepped out of their kiss.

Xander's brows wrinkled before he chuckled nervously. "You trippin' me out right now, but I'mma let it slide because I'm hanging out with my baby today... and ain't nothing about to bring me down."

That queasy feeling was washing over her again. She swallowed it back, then clenched her jaw.

"Where should I put this candle?"

Before she could part her lips to speak, he said, "I'll just leave it here."

Xander placed the bag on the table near the front door, then started walking toward the bathroom on her main floor.

"I'mma use the bathroom real quick and then we can head out," he said, gesturing in front of himself.

Rylee was slow to register what he'd said and where he was going.

The second she recalled that the pregnancy test was sitting on the vanity in that bathroom... it was too late.

"Xander, wait—"

Her words were cut short when she saw Xander disappear into the bathroom.

She didn't move. Felt stuck to the spot where she stood.

It didn't take long for Xander to step back out... holding the pregnancy test in his possession.

All he did was hold it up at first before asking, "Rylee?"

Her breaths were heavy now.

"Is... is this yours, baby?"

Rylee's shoulders fell at the sight of the test in his hand.

When she'd taken the test and saw the two lines, it was real. But seeing Xander holding it... made her reality physically shift.

She nodded her head, and with that confirmation, she noticed Xander's eyes light up in a way she'd never seen before.

His chest started to rise and fall as he peered down at the test, then looked up at her.

A stunned laugh left him next, and there was no denying it. The man was elated.

"Yo! You're pregnant?" He laughed, bringing his fist to his mouth. "We're gonna have a baby?!"

Rylee thought her heart had dropped when she saw the test. But his reaction?

That made it crash through the floor.

Because...

She didn't mean to say what she said next.

It just... slipped out.

Like a secret she'd been holding in her throat that pushed past her lips before she could stop it.

"I don't know if I'm keeping it."

It was like a thought... but in sound.

And as it came into her mind and toppled out of her mouth, falling to the hardwood floor like cement, it knocked the smile right off Xander's lips.

"Wait... what?" Xander blinked twice. "What do you mean?"

Rylee inhaled a breath through her mouth, then let it out through pursed lips.

"I... *umm...*"

The silence between them was deafening.

Rylee swore she could hear her heart beating in her ears.

"Rylee—"

"I *never* planned on having three kids."

Xander closed his eyes and squeezed them tight.

"I'm still grieving," she added. "And I *finally* feel like I can love you for real."

Xander blinked a few more times in response.

"And... and now I have to think about... *this.*"

"Think about what?" he asked, low. "What... *what* is there to think about?"

Rylee didn't respond. She couldn't.

Even if she tried, her tongue felt like it weighed one hundred pounds in her mouth.

"Okay, aight."

Xander ran a hand down his mouth and released a small laugh.

"I get it, I get it." He nodded. "It's a lot. And it's kind of crazy."

She shook her head. "Xander..."

"But I got you," he cut in. "I got you. You *know* that. I love you. I love your kids."

He closed the distance between them and pressed a hand to her stomach.

"And I'mma love this one too. On God."

Her heart ached in her chest so much she had to drop her head, feeling the warmth of his palm against her belly.

His touch somehow eased the queasiness in that moment.

"You don't have to do it alone, baby." He shook his head. "You don't ever have to do any of this alone. I got you. And I want this, Rylee. I really, *really* do."

She stood there for a moment, hearing him, feeling him.

And still... she shook her head, biting at her bottom lip.

"Xander, it's not about that."

Rylee locked eyes with him and stepped away from his touch.

"You can't carry this for me."

His chest seemed to cave at that.

"Snoop…"

The defeat in his voice made Rylee's throat go dry. But she shook her head harder, fighting off the feeling so she could stand her ground.

"Xander, as much as I hear you and as good as what you're saying sounds right now… this decision is mine to make."

His eyes bugged the moment the words left her mouth.

He stepped back like the words had hands and punched the air from his chest.

"I mean… shit. I know it's your choice," he acknowledged, low. "But damn, Rylee… I thought we were building something. I thought we were doing this whole thing together."

She didn't answer.

"So, what?" he asked. "You… you weren't gonna tell *me* or something?"

Rylee squeezed her eyes closed and pressed her hands to her face, turning away.

"You were just gonna decide this on your own?"

Her hands were on either side of her face, head spinning again.

Because… yeah, she was going to keep it to herself. Never tell him. And likely hate herself for it. But in the short time between realizing she was pregnant to Xander's arrival, she *had* considered never telling him.

"Wow," she heard him whisper behind her. "Wow."

She turned to face him again, seeing him shake his head and back away.

He pointed toward the front door behind him with his thumb.

"I gotta go."

"Xander—"

"Nah." He shook his head slowly, eyes still on hers. "I can't stay here while you *think* about *not* having my baby, Rylee."

He scoffed then inhaled an audible breath, turning toward his sneakers and pushing his socked feet into them.

"Xander, you don't have to go."

"Yeah, I do," he said, not looking her way as he pulled open her front door without a second thought.

And before she could call his name again, or say anything...

He walked out, closing her door behind him.

XANDER

XANDER LEANED back in the driver's seat after putting his truck in park. His eyes climbed the stairs of his mother's daycare, the glass front door sparkling as always, visibly displaying the daycare's name in colorful letter blocks. Future Seeds Daycare.

He had no plans to stop by here today.

At that hour, Rylee should've been beside him in the passenger seat, the two of them singing off-key to 90s R&B on their way to lunch like he'd planned.

He also had no plans to hear that she was pregnant.

And of course, not that she had no plans to keep it.

The mental recap of everything that happened over the past eight minutes had him dropping his head to his steering wheel. He was experiencing so many emotions at once. Too many. He had no idea how to sort through them.

He was going to be a father... or was he?

"Shit," he sighed, scratching the top of his locs before unhooking his seatbelt to step out.

He could think of no other place to go.

This wasn't something he could talk to with his friends.

Xander needed his mama.

As he climbed the steps to the front door, he did a quick scan of the front yard, like always.

From the time he was a teenager working with his mother at the daycare whenever school let out, Xander had been just as responsible for Future Seeds as his mother, Michelle.

She never asked him to be... he just was.

Xander was a man of service. Couldn't help it.

Plus, it brought him so much joy, helping his mother and being around children.

To him, a child's life was fragile and one of the most important things in the world. They were the future, every last one of them, with each experience shaping who they'd become. So Xander made it his mission to make every interaction with a child a phenomenal one, knowing it could leave a lasting mark. One they might carry forward, and one day, pay forward too.

He peeked over the brownstone's railing at the glass koi pond, ensuring all the fish were still swimming happily, which they were.

The moment Xander pushed open the brownstone's doors, his sound space became filled with the symphony of Future Seeds Daycare.

There was crying.

Toys clattering.

Lullabies being played low from a Bluetooth speaker.

"Oh, thank God," Xander heard to his right.

He glanced that way to find Ms. Carla, one of Future Seeds' caregivers, bouncing a wailing baby in her arms while patting his back.

"He won't stop fussing," Ms. Carla explained, closing the space between them. "Teething. His mother said he's been fussy since the night before. We gave him ibuprofen but now he's just restless."

Xander quickly peeled off his bomber jacket, tossing it onto a nearby chair. He rubbed his hands together briskly to warm them up, rid them of the winter air he'd just stepped out of.

"Do what you do," Ms. Carla said, handing the crying baby off to him. "I'm gonna go fix his crib so I can put him down for a nap."

"My child just walked in here and you already putting him to work," Michelle, Xander's mother, joked from behind the counter.

"Aw, it's aight," Xander said to his mother, lowering his attention to the baby boy. "What you crying for, anyway?" He pressed the baby to his chest and patted his pamper in a soft rhythm. "You gon' be able to eat solid foods once all them teeth come in. Quit trippin'."

The crying continued, but then... within seconds, it gradually got quieter until all that remained were soft whimpers and far less noise.

"Mr. Baby Whisperer does it again," Ms. Carla joked, smiling while folding her arms over her chest. "I'mma run upstairs, get his crib ready, and will be back for him."

"Take your time," Xander said low, continuing to rock the baby who had now allowed his heavy eyes to close.

"*Hmph*," Michelle huffed, then laughed, leaning an arm on the counter. "You sure I don't got no grandbabies running around this city somewhere? You too good with this, I swear."

He glanced at her and scoffed.

Michelle jerked her head back, then lowered her attention to her wristwatch. "I'm surprised you're here."

"Didn't plan to be," he confirmed low, lifting the baby—now asleep—to his shoulder. Xander bounced the baby slowly as he approached his mother behind the counter. "When Ms. Carla comes back to get him, I gotta talk to you."

Michelle squinted her eyes, analyzing her son.

Xander knew that look. His mother had worn it his entire life, whenever she was trying to get to the bottom of something before he even said a word.

"Well, all right." She gestured upstairs toward her office. "I'll be up there when you're ready."

Xander nodded as he turned, continuing to bounce the sleeping baby.

His mind wandered to moments ago at Rylee's brownstone.

Walking into that bathroom.

Seeing that pregnancy test.

He thought he was seeing things at first. Probably wouldn't have even known how to read it if the box wasn't right there, displaying what a positive pregnancy test should look like.

He sucked his teeth when his heart ached at the words she spoke to him.

*"This decision is mine to make."*

He bit at his bottom lip, lost cadence in the bouncing of the baby, but quickly regained it when the boy started to stir.

It was kind of ironic... him being able to calm other people's children with ease... but unable to find any calm in his own life in that moment.

As expected, Ms. Carla returned and skillfully retrieved the sleeping child. Xander and Ms. Carla made their way upstairs together, whispering conversation so they wouldn't wake the baby until they split off in different directions.

This daycare was like Xander's second home.

His first real job, if you let him tell it.

He loved Future Seeds, loved what it represented—a place in the community where he'd watched so many neighborhood children grow up.

So many of them had gone off to high school and college, and it always warmed his heart to see them pop back in, their baby pictures still on the bulletin board his mother kept by the door.

Xander walked through the open door of his mother's office.

He found her sitting behind her desk, her glasses resting on the bridge of her nose as she typed on the keyboard of her computer.

He stopped in front of the couch she kept in her office and dropped himself onto the cushion, sighing loudly.

Michelle removed her glasses and turned her chair away from the computer to focus on her son.

Xander dropped his head back against the couch and turned to look her way.

"You look like someone stole your smile."

*"Hmph."*

"Who I gotta go see and fuck up?"

Xander hollered a laugh. A laugh he really did need in that moment.

He shook his head a second later and said, "I'm just tired."

Obviously not true.

But there was no way he could get right to it after she said that.

Although Rylee's words had cut like a hot knife to his heart, he loved her... and he loved that his mother loved her too.

But this?

It was eating him up.

And it had only just happened moments ago.

"*Mmm-hmm.*" Michelle leaned back in her seat and folded her arms. "Tired, huh? You only come here on your days off to fix something or when you need to talk. So I know it gotta be more than you being tired, Xander. What's up?"

He inhaled a deep breath and puffed his cheeks as he exhaled.

She sucked her teeth. "Boy, if you don't..."

He snickered.

"Out with it."

Xander sat up, then ran his hand across the back of his neck and said, "Rylee's pregnant."

Michelle gasped so loud, her reaction echoed around the room.

"What?!" she shouted, her smile so big Xander could see all of her teeth. "Oh, baby!" she squealed. "I'm so happy... *ahh*! That's *awesome* news—"

"She might not keep it."

"Oh," she whispered, blinking a few times before nodding quickly. "Oh... okay."

Her chest visibly rose and fell a few breaths before she closed her eyes, inhaled deep, and sat up.

"Well, damn," she exhaled. "I have never experienced such a high and low in my emotions in one breath in my life."

Xander scoffed a laugh. "Tell me about it."

"Well…" She shook her head and waved her hands in the air. "What do you mean by she might not keep it?"

Xander told her everything that had transpired. Him showing up at Rylee's home, walking into her bathroom, and finding the pregnancy test.

He then took his time retelling the conversation in which Rylee told him it was her choice what she might do… and that she might not keep their baby.

"She said she's still grieving," Xander added, pinching the space between his eyes. "Said she never planned on three kids." He stopped to lick his lips and bite his bottom one. "I told her I'd handle it, that I wanted this baby, but… she said it's her decision."

He squeezed his eyes closed. The recollection of her stating it was her choice cut just as deep as actually hearing her say the words.

"And she's right." He forced a nod. "I *know* she's right. But damn, Ma." He lifted his gaze to his mother, who now looked so sad for him. "How can I live with that?"

Xander was up on his feet, hands at the top of his locs as he started pacing.

"I *want* this family," he confessed, stopping to look at her. "I want her, *so* bad. But she's so loyal to Lennox, which I love and hate at the same fucking time because sometimes I feel like I'm fighting a ghost… and getting my ass handed to me every time."

Michelle sighed, then ran her fingers through her pressed hair.

She pointed up at him and told him, "First, I'm gonna let that language slide because this is a moment which justifies it… but you gon' get no more *fucks* out that mouth around here."

He sucked his teeth. "You said *fuck* earlier."

"I don't give a *fuck* what *I* said," she snapped back, which made him laugh. "*You* don't say it. Watch what I *do*, not what I *say*."

He held his hands up in mock surrender.

"Second," she exhaled, standing from her desk. "You're not fighting a ghost, baby."

Michelle closed the distance between herself and her son. She took his hand and added, "You're loving a woman who's been through hell. There's a very big difference."

Xander's shoulders sank at that, because yes, his mother was right.

Rylee had experienced a level of heartbreak he always wished he could take from her whenever he looked into her eyes.

If he could bear the pain she clearly carried on her heart, he would. Without question.

Michelle guided Xander back to the couch, taking a seat beside him and placing her hand on his knee.

"You said you love her, right?"

He nodded, eyes on the carpet. "Very much."

"Then let her feel what she needs to feel."

Xander looked at his mother, and she gave him a sweet smile while squeezing his knee.

"Grief..." She shook her head. "That *thang* doesn't have a time-line. You know that better than most, being in your line of work, and just from experience."

Xander ran his tongue across his teeth, his mind playing back some of the most heartbreaking scenarios he'd found himself in as a firefighter.

There weren't many, but the tragedies he'd had the unfortunate opportunity of being in the center of... they'd truly stolen a little life from him.

But really, nothing compared to growing up without a father who died from gun violence.

"When I lost your father," Michelle continued, "I could not be bothered with anyone. I just could not do it, so I totally get where Rylee is coming from. I probably would've considered what she's considering if I'd gotten pregnant when I believed I was done with children."

She turned to face him fully.

"So, look..." Michelle paused to press her hands together, like she was about to pray, dropping her head to gather her breath before continuing.

"If that woman decides she can't have the baby..."

Xander sucked his teeth and looked away, shaking his head. He didn't even want to consider what it would be like if Rylee actually decided to go through with it.

Michelle was quick to take his head in her hands, pressing her palms to either side of his face.

"Xander. Xander," Michelle said until he looked at her again. "If she decides *not* to have it, real love means you don't hold it against her."

He shook his head. "That's easier said than done, though, Ma. Come on..." Xander inhaled a stuttered breath.

Michelle moved her hands off his face and placed a hand to his chest. "Xander—"

"I already see that kid in my head," he interjected, tapping his temple with his fingertip. "I see Rylee with a belly."

He smiled next. "Nova rubbing it, LJ talking to it." He closed his eyes, allowing himself to enjoy that vision for what it was worth. "I can't unsee that. I just... I can't."

Michelle scooted closer on the couch and pressed a hand to the side of his face. "Then, baby, pray on it... and love her *anyway*. You hear me? Love her anyway."

Xander swallowed back the lump forming in his throat and looked away, needing to blink back the tears pooling in his eyes.

He sniffed, then dropped his head back against the neck of his mother's couch, closing his eyes.

Michelle was quick to wrap her arms around him and lean his head against her chest.

And even though Xander was grown, in his mother's hug he felt like a kid again.

He felt safe, like everything would really be okay.

Xander melted into her embrace the way only a grown man who's run out of strength could melt into his mother's arms.

"You can't fix this for her, Xander. You just gotta be there when she's ready to talk, you know?"

Xander nodded. It was the right thing to do. He also nodded because he couldn't see himself doing anything else but being there for Rylee whenever she needed him.

"Because that's what real men do. And baby, you are a real man." Michelle nodded. "And I know she knows that."

Xander spent almost half an hour at his mother's daycare, the two of them talking a little more until the weight on his chest felt a little lighter.

Although he still felt down about everything that had happened at Rylee's home...

He at least had a plan.

He would wait.

And pray.

Wait for her to let him know when she was ready to talk, and pray that she wouldn't make her decision without speaking with him again.

Xander was making his way down the stairs and heading to the front door when he passed the room where a group of toddlers were napping.

He spotted one of the toddlers, a little girl, poking her head up and immediately gripping the crib railing when she saw him.

He pressed a finger to his lips and gestured for her to lay back down, which she didn't obey.

He snickered to himself as he entered the room, waving at one of the caregivers who was just about to stand up to attend to the little girl.

"It's time to nap, pretty girl," he said to her, pinching her cheek.

Xander helped her back onto her back, lifted the pacifier that had fallen from her mouth and was laying on the mattress. After giving her the pacifier and placing a stuffed animal beside her, he covered her and pressed a hand to her forehead.

"Sleep, sleep," he whispered, before turning to leave, waving at the caregiver once more as he exited the room.

The moment he stepped out the door and closed it behind him, he stood on the stoop, inhaling the cold Brooklyn air and staring out at the tree-lined neighborhood in front of him.

He had no idea what would come next after all of this.

But he knew one thing for certain…

He wasn't giving up.

Not on Rylee.

And definitely not on the idea of her having their baby.

RYLEE

"AH!" Mrs. Walker shouted, pressing her hands to her chest. "Look how big you two have gotten."

Rylee snickered as she ushered Nova and LJ through the Walkers's front door and right into the arms of their grandmother, Ivy Walker.

"Hi, Grandma," Nova and LJ greeted in unison, rushing up to her.

"Oh!" Mrs. Walker laughed as both children wrapped their arms tightly around her. "I can barely breathe, but who cares about breathing, right?"

Rylee snickered.

They'd just arrived at the Walkers' residence for an impromptu visit. Not unusual. Rylee often stopped by with the kids so they could spend time with their grandparents, and the Walkers were always okay with it.

"Rylee, my baby." Mrs. Walker extended her arms wide.

Rylee walked right into Mrs. Walkers's embrace, closing her eyes in their hug.

"You always make it seem like you haven't seen us in years, when we were just here last week."

Mrs. Walker chuckled, playfully slapping Rylee on the back before stepping out of their hug.

"I knew I heard my favorite little voices down here."

Rylee's eyes landed on Mr. Walker—who she and everyone else called Cy. His locs, now more silver than black, swayed behind him as he made his way toward her and the kids.

"I wasn't expecting y'all," he said to Rylee, wrapping his arms around her first before crouching his tall frame down to hug the children.

"Yeah," Rylee replied, her voice breaking a little. "I needed to come and talk to you guys and figured you'd want to see your favorite people too."

The Walkers exchanged a glance before looking back at her.

Rylee bit inside her cheek and looked away.

She'd just come from her first prenatal appointment a few hours ago. She was lucky enough to be seen, and luckier that her doctor had a slot open.

That's when she learned the baby was still in its earliest weeks.

She'd even heard the baby's heartbeat.

But the night before that, she sat in the middle of her bed with Lennox's photo in front of her, eyes fixed on the glass—on his eyes— talking to him.

*"I have a doctor's appointment tomorrow, and going will make all of this real,"* Rylee whispered to the photo in front of her. *"What would you say to me right now?"*

*She swore she felt Lennox's steady, comforting presence lingering in the air the way it did on the good days—warm, quiet, and familiar.*

*"I'm not prepared for any of this... at all, Lenny."*

*The kids were asleep in their rooms, the brownstone quiet. Rylee's bed was still made, and she was showing no signs of pushing back the covers to drift off to sleep. She wasn't tired. If anything, she was too awake for this late hour. But her mind was inundated with questions, all centered on the baby growing inside of her.*

*"And through it all, I can't help wondering what you would tell me,"*

*she admitted, lifting the photo now and brushing her finger down his face. "Because I think I know what I want, but then I don't know if you'd want me to want that. I don't feel I know how to honor you and still move forward."*

*She placed the photo back on the bed and tossed herself onto her pillow, eyes fixed on the ceiling now.*

*And maybe that was what scared her most...*

*Wanting this baby.*

*And wanting Xander there with her right now, too.*

"Well," Mr. Walker began, focusing on the children. "Who wants to paint downstairs in the studio so Mommy can have that talk with Grandma?" He looked to his wife, then Rylee, and winked. "...and Grandma can tell me all about it after?"

Rylee giggled.

"Me! Me!" both Nova and LJ shouted, jumping up with their hands raised.

"Perfect," Mr. Walker replied, nodding toward the basement where he kept his art studio. "I've got everything set up already. Let's go."

As they cleared out, Mrs. Walker nodded toward the kitchen and led the way, Rylee following close behind.

The Walkers' brownstone was her second home. It was a place she'd spent a lot of her life, from the time she learned to walk to that moment there, with the children whose father was a man she'd been friends with since birth.

The residence breathed artistry. Mrs. Walker's elegance danced through the décor, with soft linens and textured upholstery, while Mr. Walker's wild color splashes—in both paint and spirit—nailed their personalities to the walls. Literally.

They were artists... Mrs. Walker, a retired ballerina turned studio owner, and Mr. Walker, an acclaimed portrait and landscape artist whose work was displayed across New York City.

For a brownstone, it was surprisingly airy. With an open floor plan, velvet furniture, and larger-than-life windows.

Rylee loved it here. Loved it even more because she got to see pieces of Lennox everywhere... because everywhere in this home held memories of her and Lennox's time spent here, from childhood right up until his death.

"Coffee?" Mrs. Walker asked as Rylee settled into a seat at the kitchen table.

Rylee smiled. "I'll take some tea. Anything you got should be fine."

"Tea?" Mrs. Walker folded her long arms and leaned her lower back against the counter opposite the table. "*Now* I'm worried."

Rylee scoffed a laugh.

"My biggest coffee drinker in the family is asking for tea." Mrs. Walker winked as she rounded the island, heading for the stove. "Luckily for us, I just made some tea shortly before you got here, so the water's still hot in the kettle."

"Perfect timing," Rylee said softly, running her hand along the surface of the table.

She traced a small stain on the wood, her mind drifting. She remembered exactly how it got there... from the science project she and Lennox did back in middle school. His mother had told them to work in the living room, but of course they didn't listen. The vinegar and baking soda from their volcano had eaten into the table. The Walkers were able to salvage most of the surface, but that one spot remained. Stubborn... just like them.

"So," Mrs. Walker said, placing the tea in front of Rylee. "What's going on, baby girl?"

Rylee tucked her lips into her mouth and rubbed them together.

"You call me on a Tuesday and tell me you need to talk." Mrs. Walker reached across the table, taking Rylee's hand. "I'm silently panicking."

Rylee closed her hand over Mrs. Walker's, holding it tightly. Her eyes filled with tears she had to sniff back.

Mrs. Walker tightened her hold too and pushed her chair in closer.

"Rylee, baby, what's up? Talk to me."

Rylee exhaled, lips trembling slightly. "I'm pregnant."

Mrs. Walker gasped, her jaw dropping, the corners of her mouth curling into a stunned smile.

"Oh my *God*!" Mrs. Walker gripped Rylee's other hand, squeezing both tight. "You're gonna be a mama again?!"

Rylee's head tilted to one side. Her brows furrowed. She blinked.

"You're not upset?" she asked, eyes darting across Mrs. Walker's.

Mrs. Walker blinked hard and pressed her hand to her chest with a sharp inhale.

"Upset? Why on earth would I be upset, Rylee?! *This* is amazing."

And just like that, the waterworks started up again. Rylee didn't know what was making her cry more—the fact that she was pregnant when she hadn't planned to be... the fact that Mrs. Walker was genuinely happy for her... or the fact that, in every sense of the word, this pregnancy was forcing her to move on from Lennox.

And she wasn't sure she was ready to.

Her doctor had confirmed the time window of conception. Since she and Xander used condoms most of the time—but didn't on the day he showed up to comfort her on the anniversary of Lennox's death—she knew that had to be when it happened.

And that made her cry even harder.

"Oh, Rylee." Mrs. Walker twisted in her seat to reach for the tissue dispenser on the island behind her. "If you don't stop all this crying, girl!"

Rylee laughed, taking the tissue from Mrs. Walker's hand to dab at her eyes.

"Why are you so upset?" Mrs. Walker asked, still holding tight to her hand. "Why would you think *I'd* be upset?"

"Because I'm pregnant and it's not..."

Rylee let the words trail off as she dropped her chin to her chest.

"And it's not Lennox's?" Mrs. Walker finished for her.

Rylee swallowed hard and nodded.

"Oh, Rylee," Mrs. Walker whispered, lifting her hand and kissing it twice. "Baby, you've already given me two beautiful grandchildren. And now you're giving me another one I can't wait to love just as much and as hard as these two."

Rylee lifted her eyes to Mrs. Walker and saw her smiling.

She could always see Lennox in Mrs. Walker's eyes, just like she saw Lennox in LJ. It was one of the many reasons she always came to this house. To see Lennox's parents... and to see Lennox in them. He resembled them both.

"Lennox would've been thrilled," Mrs. Walker said with a nod. "Even more than *me*."

Rylee sniffed. "I don't know. I *want* to believe that, but... I just don't know."

Mrs. Walker gently ran her thumb along the back of Rylee's hand.

"Rylee, Lennox was your friend before anything else. That never changes. And any friend worth their name wants to see the people they love happy, not sad. That's true in life and in death."

Rylee kept her gaze locked on Mrs. Walker's. She wanted to believe her. She knew what Mrs. Walker was saying was right, but... her heart just couldn't catch up to that truth.

"I'm struggling," Rylee whispered. "I'm struggling to accept everything. Things just... they seem to just be happening, you know?"

Mrs. Walker nodded but said nothing. Just listened.

"Lennox's death. LJ's birth. Meeting Xander..." Rylee smiled softly through her tears. "Now *this*. Pregnant. Again?! Like what the hell?"

She kissed her teeth and shook her head. "I'm struggling because as much as I try to hang on to what used to be, life just keeps pushing me forward."

"Because you're *living*, Rylee. And that's a fantastic thing." Mrs. Walker squeezed her hand. "It's a necessary thing."

"I know," Rylee whispered. "I just... I want to make sure I'm doing *everything* right. I want to make sure the children remember Lennox. I want to make sure *I* remember Lennox."

They sat in silence for a moment before Rylee added, "I want this baby. My first reaction when I found out I was pregnant was no… but an hour after realizing it was real, that it happened, I wanted the baby. And I'm struggling because I already love it. I love the baby's father… but I'm scared that me loving all these things that aren't Lennox is me getting closer and closer to forgetting him—"

"That will never happen, Rylee," Mrs. Walker interjected, shaking her head. "If that's what you're worried about, let me tell you… it will never happen. You will *always* have Lennox in your heart."

"But I feel like I'm betraying him."

"Rylee, my son would have been beside himself excited for you. You *have* to know that. And if he were here, he'd tell you himself."

Rylee squeezed her eyes closed, a single tear slipping down her cheek.

"Lennox isn't gone from your heart just because someone else is in it too."

Rylee lifted her eyes to Mrs. Walker.

"This baby is not a betrayal, Rylee." Mrs. Walker's smile gradually grew. "It's a continuation. And I am so very grateful I'm here for this leg of your journey, baby. Thrilled."

Mrs. Walker stood from her seat and rounded the kitchen table. Rylee stood too, wrapping her arms around her and hugging her tight. Mrs. Walker left a kiss on Rylee's head, and in that moment… that very simple moment, along with Mrs. Walker's simple words…

Something shifted for Rylee.

For the better.

* * *

Rylee giggled to herself as she watched Nova dance to a classic R&B track from the '80s.

Now at her parents' house—just a day after visiting the Walkers—Rylee found herself smiling as Nova danced in her grandparents' living room. Rylee had called her mother the moment she returned home, asking if it would be fine to stop by the house Rylee had called home from birth to eighteen. It was also the house where her water broke with Nova, when Rylee stayed with her parents after a fight with Lennox made her leave the brownstone he'd bought for them to live in together. The same brownstone she lived in now.

So much had changed since that night Rylee ran into her parents' room to tell them her water had broken.

So much life had been lived... lost... and now, new life was forming inside her.

She pressed her hand to her belly, sitting up in her seat and clearing her throat.

Déjà vu.

Rylee remembered the same throat-clearing she'd done to get her parents and Lennox's parents' attention at Lennox's condo in the city on his birthday. Where she'd told them she was pregnant. That *they* were pregnant.

And tonight, she would be doing it all again... alone.

"So," Rylee voiced from the seat on her parents' couch, "I have news."

She gained her parents' attention as Nova and LJ remained caught up in their own world, dancing to the track and laughing hysterically in their kid-like distraction.

"I'm pregnant."

Revealing it this time came easier. Everything had felt easier after speaking with Lennox's mother.

Her parents' faces lit up. Rylee's father, Gannon, pointed at her mother, Claudia, and they both hollered, "I knew it!"

Rylee's brows wrinkled as she laughed. "Excuse me?"

"Chile," her mother drawled with her Southern accent, "soon as you scrunched up your nose at the smell of my cornbread, I knew somethin' was cookin', and not just in our oven."

"*Mmm-hmm*," Gannon added, standing from his seat on the

floor. "*That* and her eating all the food she did manage to eat then asking—"

"Did I just eat all of this?" Claudia finished, tossing her head back in a laugh. "Aw, baby, congratulations!"

Her parents sat on either side of her, pulling her into a big hug and holding her tight.

Nova and LJ, still dancing moments earlier, stopped to see what was going on with the adults.

"Another blessing," Gannon acknowledged, pulling his daughter close to press a kiss to Rylee's forehead.

"And another little heartbeat," Claudia added, resting her head on Rylee's shoulder. "Shoot, I wish Xander was here for me to give him a hug too."

Rylee sighed.

"I haven't been really good to Xander. Especially after getting the news."

Claudia sat up to look at her daughter.

"I panicked when I found out," Rylee admitted, watching as her children busied themselves with the toys their grandparents had brought out as soon as they arrived. "Thought about not having it—"

"Rylee," Gannon exhaled.

"I know," Rylee whispered. "I know, Dad. It's just... I never *planned* for this. I thought Nova and LJ were it for me. Then, I was in my feelings, wondering how Lennox would feel about it—"

"Lennox would want this for you." Gannon nodded, wrapping his arm around her shoulder. "That's *how* he would feel about it."

Claudia nodded.

"Ivy said the same thing."

"Ivy!" Claudia shouted. "What you mean Ivy said the same thing? I know you are *not* telling me you done told *my* best friend before *me!*"

Rylee tucked her lips into her mouth as Gannon chuckled under his breath.

"You know what, whatever." Claudia giggled. "Not as big of a deal as I'd really like to make it."

Rylee snickered.

"I'm way too happy about this news." Claudia pressed a hand to Rylee's belly. "My baby is having another baby. We're gonna have to have Xander over so we can *really* celebrate."

That thought stayed with Rylee all the way home.

She was pregnant.

Rylee knew that before tonight... and last night... but these were the first nights she didn't feel terrible about it.

As soon as she and the children walked through the door, Nova raced up the stairs—headed to her room, Rylee assumed—with LJ close behind.

Rylee's brows wrinkled as she laughed to herself.

"Where are they going?"

On the car ride home, Rylee had shared the news directly with the children. Although they were present when she told her parents she was pregnant, Rylee wanted to tell them herself.

*"Did you two hear what I told Grandma Claudia and Grandpa Gannon tonight?"*

*Rylee peeked into the rearview mirror, meeting the eyes of her children in the backseat.*

*"About the baby?" Nova asked in her little voice.*

*Rylee smiled to herself as her eyes scanned the road in front of them. Nova was always so sharp. Nothing ever got past her, so although she'd shown no indication she was listening at the Daniels', she was definitely tuned in.*

*"Yes." Rylee nodded. "Mommy is gonna have a baby with Uncle Xander."*

*The words felt so weighted on her tongue. So unreal, too. But it was happening. And she was excited about it... finally not feeling guilty for being excited.*

*"Cool," Nova said, a smile playing on her lips.*

*"Yeah," LJ echoed, looking to his sister and then to Rylee. "Cool."*

Rylee figured that was it and knew it would be the first of many conversations. And she was ready... and nervous too.

Nova was too young to understand when Rylee was pregnant with her baby brother. With this new baby, Rylee knew there would be talks to have. Probably even questions the children would ask the more she started to show.

Rylee pressed her hand to her belly and smiled.

She paused near the entryway, taking a moment to let it all settle in.

She was going to have another baby. And for the first time since the test... it felt good.

She had so many questions. So many curiosities. The one she couldn't wait to answer was... how would a new baby fit into the lives she'd already created for her two children?

"I hope you two washed your little hands," Rylee called as she started ascending the stairs, en route to Nova's room where she figured they'd be. "Because germs just *love* waiting for the right time to escape into tiny little bodies of children who didn't wash their hands after coming in from outside."

As soon as Rylee reached the top stairs, she heard Nova speaking. Instead of walking naturally, she tiptoed to the room, pressing her back to the wall that separated Nova's room from LJ's.

"I'm gonna give the baby my dolls," Nova revealed, placing a few of her dolls onto her bed. "Then I'm gonna make room on my bed so the baby can sleep with me."

"I want the baby to sleep with me, though," LJ pouted.

Rylee snickered to herself. In that moment, she didn't interrupt. She just listened to her babies discuss the baby who wasn't even here yet. Already accepting the idea of a new sibling.

"I have to show you how to hold the baby before the baby comes." Nova scooped up one of her dolls and motioned at LJ to move closer to her. "Sit like this."

Nova held her arms in a cradle, encouraging LJ to do the same.

All Rylee did was smile as she peeked inside, watching them.

Nova placed the doll in LJ's arms, adjusting the position of his little hands.

It wasn't the right way to hold a baby, at all, but Rylee knew they had time to practice. Plus, she was too busy enjoying watching her children be so open to the idea of a new baby entering their lives.

"Good," Nova approved with a nod.

Rylee had to cover her mouth to keep from laughing too loud. Nova was already a big sister, but clearly working on being the ultimate big sister in training.

In the next breath, Rylee's eyes welled up. She instinctively pressed her hand to her stomach, knowing that her decision was now grounded in love and reassurance.

The baby was already so loved.

She stepped forward and into the room, going straight for LJ. She lifted him up and sat him on her lap while reaching for Nova.

Rylee pressed a big kiss to Nova's cheek and then to LJ's, hugging them tight to her.

"You're gonna be a *great* big sister. You know that, right?"

"Yup!" Nova said. "I know."

Rylee giggled.

"How about me, Mommy?" LJ quizzed. "Will I be a good big brother?"

"Yup." Rylee nodded. "The *best* big brother that ever was, baby."

Now that everyone had been told—and everyone was excited—Rylee knew it was time to talk to Xander.

Time to let him in.

And time to celebrate... as a family.

Finally.

*thirteen*

RYLEE

RYLEE GATHERED her long braids to the top of her head, twisting them into a bun as she passed the large red fire truck.

As soon as she stepped into the firehouse, Jamal, Xander's friend and fellow firefighter, smiled big, laying the pen he wrote with on the desk he sat behind.

"Aye, Rylee!" he said, standing to his feet, immediately making his way around the desk. "What's up, lil' mama?"

He extended his arms for a hug and she walked right into them, giving him a quick embrace.

It was a Thursday, quiet, and exactly what Rylee was hoping it would be when she decided to stop by the firehouse.

"Nothing much." She playfully tapped his stomach. "Just being a creep. Thought I'd swing by my man's job unannounced. Keep him on his toes and his head on a swivel. You know the vibes."

Jamal laughed, then gestured at the stairs that led up to the kitchen.

"Well, he's up there cooking." Jamal rubbed his hand over his firehouse tee. "And thank God. Been looking forward to his chicken *all* day."

"*Mmm.*" Rylee licked her lips. "Looks like I came at the right time, huh?"

"Sure did," Jamal replied. "Head up there. I'll see you in a few."

Rylee nodded her exit and followed Jamal's direction, climbing the stairs to the kitchen.

This was the first time she was seeing Xander since everything changed. He'd given her space she hadn't asked for but that he knew she needed.

And she really did.

In that time apart, she'd done a lot of thinking, visiting Lennox's grave to facilitate that thinking, and had decided on her own that she wanted this baby.

Although getting pregnant wasn't planned, she knew it was meant to be. She said as much when she visited Lennox's grave days prior.

*"Well," she sighed, lowering herself onto the earth in front of his head- stone. She pretzeled her legs, feeling the cold grass and soil beneath her jeans, ignoring it, and finding warmth gazing at his name etched on the stone. "Dr. Grayson confirmed there's a baby in my belly again."*

*The brisk breeze in the cemetery whistled through the barren trees like it always did during the colder months.*

*"And... ummm." She pushed air through her nose. "I decided to keep it."*

*Rylee bit at her bottom lip, squeezing her eyes.*

*"I've thought for days about everything," she continued. "Everyone is happier than I thought they'd be. I've imagined what life is about to look like. Me, three kids?" Rylee shook her head. "And I don't know. The more I imagine it, the less scary it feels. And believe me, it was terrifying at first. The timing, the grief, the thought of starting over when I thought I was finally settling into this new normal without you. Crazy, right?"*

*She stared forward, eyes locking in on the laser-etched photo of Lennox on the headstone.*

*"I'm in love with him, Lenny," she whispered. "I'm so in love with him."*

*Rylee snickered, shaking her head. "Can you believe that? Me, who had sworn off all you fools only to find one that is nowhere near a fool I've ever dated. And now, my ass is pregnant."*

*She dropped her attention to her stomach, pressing her hand there over her coat.*

*"You never listen," she chastised, lifting her eyes again. "You always do what you want to do and how you want to do things. Because, Lenny, I told you to give me a sign. And you, being you... still had to do it your way. A baby? Really, guy? 'Cause I know I sound crazy, but I just feel you had something to do with this."*

*She smiled, her chest swelling with hope, gratitude, and a touch of anxiety.*

*"And if you did have something to do with this..." Rylee leaned forward to press her hand to his headstone. "Thank you, Lenny."*

Conceiving on the anniversary of Lennox's death was still hard to believe for Rylee. Everything that has happened since Lennox took his last breath has been crazy, but for once, she wasn't running scared from the unpredictable and the unknown. She was ready to run towards it. Especially if Xander would be running with her.

She reached the top of the stairs, the aroma of fried chicken sizzling in a cast iron skillet stronger now on the top floor.

His cooking had been his way of filling his absence. At least that's how Rylee felt.

Even though they hadn't spoken since that day he left her brownstone after discovering she was pregnant, every few days in the afternoon, she'd hear her doorbell ring then walk her way to the door to find a Tupperware full of lunch and a yellow sticky note with a short message.

One note read...

*It's time for lunch. – Xander*

Another read...

*Time to take a break. – Xander*

It was cute. Very Xander-coded. And definitely contributed to Rylee's decision to keep what she and Xander created together.

On the other side of the long communal table stood Xander, towering over a steel stove.

Music from a Bluetooth speaker played old school hip-hop from the 90s as Rylee stopped walking for a moment, watching Xander in his element, bobbing his head to the rhythm of the song.

She took light steps in his direction, passing a fire pole and the historic red-brick walls on one side of the kitchen.

Her eyes scanned the wooden island on her way to him, her attention lingering briefly on pamphlets with Greene Gardens logos plastered on them.

Rylee switched her focus to Xander, smiling as she approached.

When she was close, she heard Xander rapping the lyrics of the song playing, his attention entirely on flipping the chicken frying in the skillet.

Rylee slipped up behind him, wrapping her arms tight around his waist.

"*Hmph*," he huffed, not at all startled. "This better be my woman, or someone's about to get a *very* awkward talking to. I swear to God."

Rylee giggled against him, pressing her lips to his back and giving him a kiss there.

Xander turned his head to peek over his broad shoulder as Rylee lifted her head to peek around to meet his eyes and noticed the exact moment his eyes lit up.

He turned around in her arms, lowered his lips, and pressed a kiss to hers.

No hesitation.

Rylee's heart felt like it turned to honey in her chest.

Xander walked her back toward the wood island and away from the sizzling chicken.

He asked softly, "What are you doing here?"

"I smelled the chicken frying from Brooklyn Heights."

He snorted a laugh, tightening his arms around her.

"I haven't heard from you," she added. "But I've been enjoying the free lunches you've been leaving on my doorstep every few days."

"*Hmph*," he huffed again, pinching her chin and pulling away for a moment to remove the chicken from the oil and to turn the fire off under the skillet.

"Figured I'd give you some space," he said, returning to his spot in front of her. "You dropped a bomb on me, Snoop. I'm kinda still recovering."

Rylee folded her lips into her mouth to rub them together.

"But it's a beautiful bomb. But *still* a bomb."

She nodded her understanding.

Rylee inhaled the air, moaning at the scent of the chicken.

"Smells good."

"It's yours," Xander offered next. He gestured behind him at the three plates full of fried chicken. "All of it. These guys don't need to eat. They'll be aight."

Rylee hollered a laugh.

"Especially, you know..." He shifted his weight from one foot to the other. "If you're eating for two. Hopefully. Even though, you know, if you're not, that's aight too. *Just* so you know."

Rylee had to blink back tears.

She could see the tension in Xander's jaw as he tried hard to swallow back his feelings.

In that moment, she felt pretty bad. He'd stayed away, given her space, but in that time she wondered, how was he coping? All she thought about was herself as she considered not having this baby. But Xander had expressed wanting the baby and was likely in mental turmoil, waiting for Rylee to tell him something. Anything.

"I *will* be eating for two," she revealed, a small smile pulling at her lips. "Probably for the next, what? Eight or so months?"

Xander exhaled a deep sigh but said nothing. Just kept his eyes on hers, his chest rising and falling a little more now.

Conversations from the floor beneath them hummed as the firefighters shouted jokes amongst themselves, all of them in their own worlds while Rylee and Xander stood in theirs.

"What if I decided to keep it?" she asked. "What would that mean to you, Xander?"

"Man, Rylee…" he said, his voice cracking before he cleared his throat, took a breath, and took her hands in his. "You'd make me the happiest man on this side of the galaxy, Snoop. For real."

Rylee smiled as she felt that familiar sting of her nose that always happened right before she started crying.

"I'd make it the easiest pregnancy you've ever had in your life," he added, stepping closer. "Love on you and protect you, the baby…" he continued, pressing a hand to her stomach. "And the kids, fiercely."

He nodded, his eyes locking on hers. "I'd honor your guy."

Rylee blinked back tears.

"I'd honor Lennox's memory. Never look to replace him, but just be worthy of the world you built with him, and always work to make it better… out of respect to him."

Xander cradled Rylee's face in his big hands.

"I'd make a very beautiful life with you and *for* you because you deserve that and so much more, Rylee."

She hadn't realized she was crying until Xander used his thumb to catch her tears.

Her bottom lip quivered as she wrapped her arms around his waist.

"I wanna have this baby," she said quietly. "With you."

Xander released his breath as if he'd been holding it for weeks, for as long as it's been since they last spoke.

He pulled her to him a breath later, wrapping his arms tightly around her and lifting her up off her feet to spin her around the open space in the kitchen.

Rylee squealed and laughed so hard, her voice echoed around them.

The moment Xander put her down on her feet, he pumped his fist in the air then covered his huge smile with it before shouting, "Aye, y'all! Rylee and I are having a baby."

The firehouse didn't miss a beat with their response. Voices erupted into cheering and clapping. A bell was ringing shortly after.

Rylee laughed to herself as she fisted his shirt to pull him close.

On cue, he lowered his lips to hers, wrapping his arms around her once more, holding her tight against him, and Rylee couldn't imagine a safer place on the planet.

A few of the firefighters made their way up to where they were, giving Xander pounds and pats on the back while pulling Rylee into soft hugs—some of them pressing hands to her stomach, excited, smiling, and making her feel like she'd just hit the jackpot.

Once the excitement settled, a lot of the guys gathered around the fried chicken, plating their lunch. Xander pulled Rylee to one side of the kitchen and away from the hungry firefighters.

"We're having a baby," he whispered on her lips, eyes closed, so very much not caring who saw him be so soft in that moment.

She smiled big, sniffing back her tears. "Yes, we are."

* * *

Hours later, in Rylee's bed, sometime after midnight, Xander and Rylee lounged together.

Rylee was on her back, head propped up on her pillows as Xander lay between her thighs, his lips showering kisses against her stomach.

One of the other firefighters insisted he switch shifts with Xander to free him up to celebrate and spend time with Rylee.

Of course Xander didn't pass up the offer. With anything else, he would have. But that day, *that* night, was definitely the exception.

The kids were asleep in their beds, Rylee's bedroom door closed. Xander had been volleying between kissing her stomach and pressing his ear to it every few beats.

Rylee giggled at him, at how excited he was.

It was beautiful.

Xander made his way up to the pillow beside her, immediately wrapping his big arm around her and pulling her to him.

Rylee closed her eyes, snuggled up beside him, loving the feel of his arms around her. Absolutely loving the moment.

In that position, Xander was back to stroking her belly, and all Rylee could do was smile.

If he was like this already, how would he be once she started showing?

Likely, absolutely beside himself.

As his long fingers moved along the landscape of Rylee's stomach, she could feel the awe and reverence in his touch already.

It was everything to her.

"You still scared?" he asked behind her, his fingers still moving softly against her.

"Terrified." She smiled. "But in the best way. And not of you, or this."

Xander moved in closer, lifting high enough to kiss her temple, then her cheek. "I'm a little scared too. I can't even lie… but thankfully, neither one of us has to do this alone, right?"

Rylee nodded. "Right."

"You don't ever have to face fear alone again, you hear me?"

"I hear you."

They were quiet again, the soft sounds of R&B playing from Rylee's Bluetooth speaker that sat on her night table to their right.

"I'mma be there for *everything*," Xander said low. "And I'mma love every part of you."

Rylee's eyes grew heavy and she smiled as she closed them.

"Love you through the grief, joy, flaws, and fears, of course."

Xander shifted in his position, his fingers steady now, hand resting on her stomach.

"I'm gonna be there for every late-night craving, every doctor's appointment," Xander continued. "Teach Nova and LJ how to be brave and soft at the same time. 'Cause you know you could be both, right?"

All Rylee did was nod.

"I'mma teach Nova and LJ how to box," he added. "Yeah. 'Cause girls should know how to fight, too. Protect themselves at all times. Yeah."

She snickered, tiredly.

"They should have a backyard, Snoop," Xander said low, sounding like he was saying that mostly to himself. "More space. A place to run and continue to grow."

His promises sounded like lullabies to her—so sweet she hadn't quite registered what he was suggesting. All Rylee knew in that moment was that any fear she had was melting away with each word he decreed.

"I'll never try to fill Lennox's shoes," Xander promised. "I'mma just... walk beside the path he helped lay and always make sure things are getting better and never worse. Not on my watch."

Rylee was seconds away from drifting off to sleep when she heard Xander say, "Our baby already has the strongest mama on the planet... and the fullest village. Believe that."

And as Xander continued speaking behind her, Rylee released all her weight onto him, her smile fixed on her lips as she drifted off to sleep.

# fourteen

XANDER - 4 MONTHS LATER...

THE SUV'S speakers were turned all the way up, bass vibrating through the floor as Xander's chief, Chief Logan, told a wild story about a family dinner gone sideways. Xander loved when the chief spent time with them, which was rare. Logan used to be captain at Xander's firehouse before the promotion but still came around when he needed a break from the brass upstairs, like that day.

Xander laughed along with the crew, but his eyes were fixed on the GPS. Half a mile until Greene Gardens.

Logan had requested a few firefighters make themselves available to visit a site in Greene Gardens the week before.

Xander had volunteered, genuinely curious about finally seeing the village he'd been viewing in brochures and that all of New York City seemed to be talking about lately. At least, that's what it seemed like.

It also seemed like every other week, someone he knew was talking about possibly buying a house in the emerging village upstate.

As they passed the *Welcome to Greene Gardens* sign, Xander took a slow sip of his coffee, eyes scanning ahead.

To his knowledge, the town was brand new, but people had already started living there and opening businesses.

It was the reason he and his crew were traveling from Brooklyn to visit on assignment.

It was late morning in the village. Xander and the other fire-fighters were there to collaborate with the developers to ensure safety compliance and proper fire-response infrastructure for their new local firehouse that would serve the area.

As soon as they crossed the first half mile past the welcome sign, Xander sat up in his seat, tuning out the conversation in the SUV.

He and his crew from the Park Slope station were temporarily assigned to assist with reviewing blueprints with project architects and engineers, making sure the design supported response times and, of course, safety codes.

But that kind of went out the window when he realized how beautiful and developed the village already was.

"Damn, they work fast, huh?" Xander noted to himself, but loud enough for a few of the guys to hear. "I thought this village was brand new. They got buildings and houses and shit."

"I'm saying," Jamal agreed beside him with a chuckle. "I was expecting deserted land and half-built properties. Scaffolding. *Anything* but *this*."

Xander blew air through his lips as his eyes continued to scan.

The area appeared to be a mixed-use village community. Looked a lot like Brooklyn to him, with the blending of brownstone charm and modern design.

Xander wasn't the only one in awe.

"Well, damn," Pauly, another firefighter, said. His eyes were pinned to his window like a kid in the backseat of his parents' mini-van. "Might have to make the move. You see that house right there?"

"Yeah," Xander whispered, his eyes glued and moving with the passing homes.

"Aye," Chief Logan called from his seat behind the wheel. "Don't be getting no ideas, you hear me? I'm not trading firefighters for no damn Greene Gardens. Talkin' about 'you see that house right there?' Y'all better *just* see it."

They all laughed, including Xander.

"Wouldn't dream of leaving you assholes," Xander said with a smirk.

Everyone laughed again.

He wouldn't dream of leaving them, but a move to Greene Gardens, like Pauly just suggested, didn't sound like a bad idea.

The guys arrived at the new firehouse site, stepping out of the SUV, all of their eyes scanning the building. The firehouse stood partially framed—steel beams, fresh cement foundation, and a banner that read *Future Home of FDNY Engine 3*.

Xander tucked in the hem of his firehouse shirt into his slacks. He and the rest of the firefighters were dressed alike, all in casual FDNY gear.

"Gentlemen," they heard behind them. Xander turned to see a smiling Black man with two women flanking him on either side. "Welcome to Greene Gardens. Y'all are early. I *like* that."

"Oh, no doubt." Xander nodded. "That's what we do."

"I'm Levi Weston," the man introduced. "I'm the lead landscape architect *and* your Greene Gardens rep today." He gestured to his right. "Over here is Presley Blake, one of our architects who's assisted with designing this firehouse. And over here..." He nodded to his left. "Is Allison Cruise, our local project manager. Thank you for coming."

All of the guys, including Xander, shook everyone's hands.

"The lead engineer is already inside," Levi informed, pointing ahead. "Let's meet him and get you guys up to speed."

At Levi's direction, they all followed him into the firehouse, both Allison and Presley sharing the blueprints to give the team an idea of what the finished building would look like.

"This is obviously not the complete schematics," Presley explained, pointing at one of the blueprints. "But it paints a pretty clear picture."

Inside, after getting introduced to the lead engineer—who

pointed out plans for two drive-through bays, crew quarters upstairs, and a community multipurpose space—they all walked the site for hands-on work.

Xander measured turning radii for the trucks parked outside. Tested hydrant water pressure with a gauge.

While checking the distance of one of the hose's reach, he noted, "If you shift that hydrant five feet, we can reach the west end faster."

The engineer nodded, lowering his attention to the folder he carried, jotting down Xander's suggestion.

"Man," Jamal said, walking alongside Xander and nudging him with his shoulder. "They should let you run this joint when it's done."

Xander snorted. "Nah, man. I'm just making sure whoever's stationed here gets it right."

"*Hmph.*" Jamal lowered into a squat to check the fire truck's tire pressure. "The way your ass was looking through the window on the way here was giving *I'm not just here for one visit.*"

Xander chuckled, shaking his head. "And why were you watching me, creep?"

Jamal let out a laugh that made his head fall back.

After the walkthrough was complete, and the others started making their way back to the SUV, Xander stood outside the fire-house for a bit, lingering, eyes scanning the area.

Jamal was inside, using the bathroom before they all hit the road and headed back to Brooklyn. Xander decided to wait out front.

He watched a couple of kids ride past the construction site on their bikes, already making memories in their first Greene Gardens summer. Their parents weren't far behind, stepping out of a café, paper cups of coffee in hand, waving back to them from down the block.

There was a row of finished brownstones and houses further down.

Xander lifted a hand to shield his eyes from the summer sun, catching sight of ivy already climbing some of the sides of those brownstones.

And in that moment, he couldn't help imagining Nova and LJ running down that same block.

Rylee with a stroller.

She was five months pregnant now, showing in the most beautiful way, and Xander loved every moment of it.

Loved how his mind—even when he wasn't trying—often had him thinking about their baby's future.

One of those future thoughts centered on housing. The brownstone in Brooklyn had only three bedrooms, and lately, Xander had been seriously thinking about what that would mean once the baby arrived.

Would he move into the brownstone?

Because there was no way Rylee and the kids would leave the brownstone to live in his one-bedroom apartment.

"Beautiful, ain't it?" he heard to his right.

Xander looked that way to see Levi smiling, eyes fixed out in front of him, and Xander smiled too while nodding.

"Y'all did y'all thing out here." Xander folded his arms over his broad chest. "I swear, when my chief told us we'd be coming out here to help with your firehouse, I thought I was coming to deserted land."

Levi laughed.

"I got the brochures and everything, but I thought that was just the finished part of the village. I can't *believe* how much ground y'all covered so fast." Xander blew air out of his mouth. "I feel like I just heard about y'all building only a couple years ago."

"We have a great principal architect." Levi nodded. "Hassani Franklin's efficient. Stern as hell about this project."

Xander laughed.

"He set project deadlines and has met each one."

"Dope."

They stood quiet for only a beat, a thought returning in that instant.

"So housing around here is open now?"

"Not all," Levi replied. "But quite a bit. As you can see, we've already got families moved in for the summer, already making a home."

"I see that," Xander replied low.

"But yeah," Levi continued. "A few units just listed last month."

"*Uh-oh*, now he's asking about properties," Xander heard Jamal comment on his approach from behind them.

Xander chuckled. "Here he go."

"You trying to move out here, Cox?" Jamal asked, stopping beside the two men.

Xander shrugged, his attention returning to the few people enjoying their day in the village. "Just asking questions."

"Well, if your questions turn into interest." Levi pushed a hand into the back pocket of his slacks, "here's a contact at our sales office. We've got a few properties opening up for sale this quarter. Some are part of the city's Good Neighbor initiative, too." Levi tapped Xander on the arm. "You'd qualify through your department."

Xander's brows shot up as he accepted the card, eyes lowering to it. "Good Neighbor? Why does that sound familiar?"

"I'm sure you've heard of it. It's a first responder incentive program. Firefighters, EMTs, teachers," Levi explained, turning to face Xander now. "They get first pick and a serious discount—up to fifty percent off—in developing zones like this."

"Oh, yeah, yeah." Xander ran his hand down his beard. "I *have* heard about that."

"The catch, though, is you gotta live there at least three years. But for someone looking to put down roots..." Levi shrugged with a smile. "It's a solid deal."

Xander nodded, his eyes returning to the card again before pocketing it. "Okay, aight. Thanks, man. I'll check it out."

"He better check it out," Jamal joked beside him, slapping a hand to his shoulder and squeezing it. "Fifty percent off? Let me get a pen and sign up my damn self."

Both Xander and Levi laughed.

After Levi walked with Xander and Jamal to the department SUV, thanking everyone for coming out to assist, the guys were back on the road and headed to Brooklyn.

As the crew struck up conversations during the ride back home, Xander stayed quiet, busy on his phone, pulling up Greene Gardens' housing site. His eyes were locked on the village, the homes, the possibilities... on the life he wanted to build.

For the first time in a long time, Xander let himself imagine staying still.

In that instance, everything just seemed... clear.

* * *

*3 months after that...*

October arrived quietly, bringing with it the eighth month of Rylee's pregnancy, and more nights with Xander sleeping under the brownstone's roof.

Xander took the steps down to the main floor of the brownstone, his eyes moving around the area, peering through the opening in the living room to see it empty.

He was half-hoping Rylee would be relaxing on the couch instead of where he already knew she was.

He scoffed, shaking his head.

She was officially in her eighth month of pregnancy and still burning the midnight oil in the basement.

Things had changed a lot since she discovered she was pregnant. Most of those changes between her and Xander. She went from telling Xander not to pop up at the brownstone to giving him a key.

*"Snoop," he said into the phone. "I'm here. Where you at?"*

*Xander was outside of the brownstone and had been knocking and ringing the bell for a good three minutes.*

*"I'm in the house."*

*"You didn't hear me ringing?" he asked next.*

*"I did," she sighed, sounding less like herself.*

*It was her second month of pregnancy, and it seemed her morning sickness wasn't just in the mornings anymore.*

*"I had my face in the toilet so, you know..."*

*He cringed. "Aw, babe."*

*"Get the key from the rock in the bush," she told him, heaving on the other end of the phone. "And keep it."*

So yeah, Xander had gotten a key to the brownstone, which to him was a major moment in time... and it was.

He went from having a key to spending more and more time at the brownstone. Stepping in to take the kids to school on his days off. Making dinner when Rylee was too sick to leave the bed.

Eventually, Rylee didn't want him to leave at all.

*His hands caressed her belly, eyes moving up to Rylee before he leaned down to press a kiss to her stomach.*

*She was six months pregnant, very much showing, and Xander was obsessed.*

*They'd learned two months prior they were having a boy, and Xander was beside himself excited. The room showed that, with baby items piling high in one corner of Rylee's bedroom.*

*"Daddy gotta bounce," he spoke to her stomach. Xander pressed a kiss there, then leaned his cheek against it, smiling when his baby boy kicked.*

*Xander peeked up at Rylee and saw a frown on her lips.*

*"Oh, don't be jealous." He smiled, climbing up to kiss her lips. "I got some of that for you, too."*

*She laughed lowly, pressing her hands to either side of his face. "It's not that."*

*Xander leaned into her touch, warmth blooming everywhere she touched.*

*"What's that face all about then?"*

*She was quiet for a moment, her thumb caressing his cheek.*

*"Can't you just... stay?"*

*He arched a brow. "Stay?"*

*"Yeah... I mean..." she said, sitting up, Xander moving out of the way and helping her press her back to the headboard. "You're here all the time when you're off anyway, so..."*

*Xander dipped his chin to meet her eyes as she focused on the bed, playing with a fold in the sheets.*

*"Snoop?"*

*She lifted her gaze to him.*

*"Are you asking me to move in?"*

*"We're about to have a baby." She shrugged. "Life's better when you're around. I miss you when you go... so, maybe I am?"*

*He blinked in response, a smile slowly pulling at his lips.*

*She smiled back, her smile tugging at his heartstrings. Beyond what she was saying, seeing her pull him more and more close after life threw them this curveball had been the best part of the experience.*

*"Yes." She nodded, inhaled a deep breath and let it go slowly. "I'm asking you to move in."*

And here Xander had been.

Tonight, he'd made dinner, the kids' choice of burgers and fries.

They were asleep in their rooms, and Xander was headed down to the basement to get their mother so she could do the same.

Plus, he had some news he was both excited and anxious to share with her.

"Snoop, let's go," Xander said the moment he reached the bottom of the basement stairs.

His woman sat in front of four computer monitors. One screen was full of scrolling numbers. Just glancing at it made his head hurt. And if she started explaining what they meant, like she always did? His brain would spin in circles, again.

The other screens were crowded with spreadsheets and news articles, all centered on stock data and stock market news.

Rylee turned in her seat, crumbs from the blueberry muffin he'd baked for her earlier stuck to the corner of her mouth.

"It's time for bed, baby," he said, reaching for the back of her chair.

She pointed at one of the monitors, her mouth too full to talk.

"Nope." Xander shook his head. "It's after ten. You told me to give you an hour. I gave you three. You need rest. Come on."

Earlier that week, they'd gone to Rylee's OB appointment together. After checking her out, Dr. Felicia Grayson had smiled and said something Xander hadn't been able to forget.

*"Your cervix is already softening, Rylee. More than we typically see this early."*

*Xander's brows had furrowed. "Is that a problem?"*

*"No, no," Dr. Grayson had said with a light laugh and a wave of her hand. "It just means her body may be getting ready to move quickly when labor starts, which is common in third pregnancies. I'd just recommend she take it a little easier from here on out. Any chance to put her feet up and enjoy this final stretch..." She'd looked at Rylee, gave her a wink. "Take it."*

At the time, Rylee had joked she had too much energy in her third trimester to do such a thing as rest. But Xander had promised himself he'd stay on top of it.

Tonight, at his insistence, she playfully rolled her eyes but couldn't help but smile, giving him her hand so he could help her up and out of her seat.

His eyes landed on her round belly in her tee. He couldn't help but smile at it before leaning around her to shut off the monitors.

He loved that Rylee was a career woman who knew how to balance. But he didn't love that she was still working as hard as she was when she wasn't pregnant. Her doctor had also suggested more rest since Rylee wasn't getting enough sleep, and as soon as Xander heard that, he'd been on her about it, holding her accountable.

"You could've given me five more minutes," she fussed as they arrived at the top of the basement stairs and Xander closed the door.

"*Mmm-hmm.*" He snickered. "I gave you three hours."

She shook her head.

They made their way up the stairs to their bedroom, Rylee stopping at the children's rooms to make sure they were sound asleep.

Her detour allowed Xander to step into their room and retrieve the photo on his phone that he wanted to show her.

She sighed as she walked into the room, shutting the door behind herself. "You think LJ was serious at dinner?"

Xander's eyes were on his phone, scrolling. "About wanting to play soccer?"

"Yeah," Rylee said, heading to the bathroom. "Because I love that boy with everything in me and think he's talented, but he got two left feet. He should stick to being a science genius. I like that one better. It's safer."

Xander snickered, stopping on the photo.

The water was running in the bathroom, Rylee quickly brushing her teeth.

Xander took a seat on their bed, his heart starting to kick up in rhythm the moment he heard the water shut off.

He turned in the bed, kept one foot on the ground and a leg on the mattress as Rylee entered the room, pulling back the covers and getting in bed.

He swallowed hard and cleared his throat as she adjusted herself, giving him her attention.

She asked, "What's up?"

"I got something I wanna show you."

She blinked twice. "Okay."

"But before I show you it," he added, "I need you to hear me when I say that nothing changes unless you want it to, aight?"

Rylee giggled nervously. "Okay…"

He bit at his bottom lip as he laid his phone on the bed.

On his phone's screen was a photo of a two-story house. Modern design, palatial, and grand.

"Wow," she exhaled, lifting his phone to get a better look at the photo. "It's beautiful. *Huge*, too."

Xander leaned in to swipe to the next few photos. "This is the neighborhood it's in."

He showed her a school, a sunrise over the park, and the half-finished firehouse that had seen more construction since he last visited three months ago.

"This is Greene Gardens," he revealed. "Remember when I said I was going out there to help with their local firehouse setup?"

She nodded. "Yeah, I remember. Bryant Greene's village. You know Lennox was close to Bryant." Rylee smiled this time, Xander's eyes falling to her dimples which he loved seeing. "That man never said *anything* about doing anything like this back then. I know Lennox would have been so beside himself had he known. Would've definitely supported the project."

Xander nodded, feeling a bit more assured. If Lennox would've supported it, that meant Rylee would approve of the village...and Xander's plans.

She jerked her head back, eyes moving off the phone and onto Xander.

"Wait, why are you showing me this?"

"Because I bought it... for us."

Rylee blinked hard. "Bought what?"

The moment Xander got back into the department's SUV after visiting Greene Gardens three months ago, he knew he wanted to buy a property there. Though he didn't reveal that to his friend Jamal while they were at the firehouse construction site, Xander was definitely interested in learning more about the village, and that program Levi Weston mentioned.

After that first visit to Greene Gardens three months ago, he hadn't been able to shake it.

One call to the contact Levi gave him turned into pre-approval paperwork, then weekend showings, and finally this house—family-friendly, close to the future firehouse, and in a neighborhood that just felt... right.

Last week, he'd signed the papers and walked out with keys in his palm and a stupid grin on his face, already picturing Rylee and the kids here.

Though he planned to travel the distance to bring the children to the school they knew in Brooklyn and to continue to work from his firehouse in Park Slope, Greene Gardens just seemed like the right choice.

That's why in early September, he made an offer and negotiations followed but moved quickly, so that by late September the offer was accepted and he entered into a contract.

In that time, he scheduled inspection, appraisal, and a final walkthrough.

A week prior, he'd closed on the house and got the keys. As he and Rylee spoke, light prep inside the house had started—which included the setting up of a nursery and getting everything in order for the surprise reveal he was doing that night, next to Rylee in their bed.

Rylee shifted in her spot on the mattress to face him. "Xander, what *exactly* did you buy?"

He swallowed hard at her reaction.

Xander knew it was risky doing it like this. A conversation first would've probably sent her spiraling before he even got the words out. Anything new had Rylee panicking, and he understood why...

He just hoped that if she could see it first—feel it—she might believe what he was still trying to convince himself of... that a new house could be good for them.

He exhaled, steadying himself. The panic he'd hoped to sidestep was already flickering behind her eyes.

"I want to raise our family there," he got straight to it. "It's peaceful. Safe. Has a lot of room to grow."

"Xander—"

"There's five bedrooms, an en suite, and two baths," he listed over her, getting completely in bed to face her. "This isn't me trying to move you. This isn't me asking you to leave your home. Your brownstone is sacred, Rylee. I *know* what it means. I would *never* take it away from you."

Rylee's bottom lip quivered. "But, Xander, baby—"

"I bought this because this program for first responders made it possible and because... I wanted to give us a maybe. A future to choose from... not a future to run to. You said it yourself. It's beautiful, right?"

"It *is*, but..." She shook her head. "I can't *just* leave this brownstone, Xander. I can't just make a home somewhere other than here. Lennox bought this for me. For Nova. To be our *only* home."

Her voice rose with each word spoken, not in anger but pure panic... something Xander was hoping to avoid.

Xander pressed a hand to her stomach. "Aight, baby, chill. Just... take it easy—"

"I need you to understand that this place is the kids and my history," she continued, chest rising. "My whole life is in *this* house, Xander."

Xander closed his eyes and took a breath. He knew it was a risk going about the home-buying process the way he did, keeping her out of it.

"He gave you a foundation." Xander nodded, opening his eyes to hers. "But this family—*our* family, Rylee—it's growing."

Xander rubbed her belly, lowering his attention to it.

"And so is our love."

Rylee was blinking her eyes quickly, eyes that were growing more and more glossy with tears as she stared back at him.

"But you know..." Xander said, reading her expression. "If this isn't what you want, we stay right where we are. No pressure. *No* timeline. The keys go back. I don't care. I only care that you feel safe."

Rylee averted her eyes, turning her head away from him.

"But I also want you to know that what I told you, about not wanting to replace Lennox? I *meant* that, Rylee," he said. "I wouldn't even dream of doing that. But *this,* right here..." Xander tapped the phone's screen. "This is about building a future, baby. LJ has a room, and so does Nova. This little guy is going to need one too, eventually—"

"We're not moving," Rylee interjected, her voice firm, finality heavy in her tone. "That's the first and *last* conversation about any of this we're going to have."

Xander's hand stilled on her baby bump.

There was a long pause between them. Too damn long of a pause, honestly.

So many things were racing through Xander's head. So many emotions. Frustration, a little anger, but overall—understanding. The reality of it all was, they could not raise another child in the brownstone. There was literally no room to do that.

"So..." He held his breath. "Send the keys back?"

Rylee shook her head, bringing her hands to her face to growl into them. "I... I don't know... I'm not saying that. I'm just *saying* I don't want to talk about this right now. And I don't know when I will."

The baby could stay in their room for the first few months of his life, but after that, he'd need his own space.

But Xander knew Rylee wasn't ready for that conversation. And because she'd made a lot of concessions without him having to ask, all he did was nod. Absorb her words.

He swallowed his disappointment, internalizing it all... including the rejection of something he saw as a dream for their family.

Xander didn't know what stung more... her no, or how fast it came.

"Aight. I understand," was how he ended the discussion.

Xander leaned in and gave her a peck on the lips before turning to his left to switch off the lamp on his side of the bed.

He reclined back on his pillow, one arm over his head, the other resting on his abs, eyes fixed on the ceiling.

He didn't know how to feel in that moment, but he knew disappointment was at the top of that list.

Rylee shut off the lamp on her side of the bed, the room gradually falling dark.

Still, Xander kept his eyes on the ceiling above them.

The bed shifted. He felt her belly first and then her head on his chest. And even though he was a little upset with her, he couldn't help the butterflies in his stomach that fluttered from her touch.

He kept his attention above them but moved his hand to her stomach, caressing it softly.

"I'm sorry," she whispered in the dark. "That was just... you just sprung that on me."

Xander remained quiet.

"The house is *beautiful*," she said, more volume in her voice. "So very beautiful. I just wish you would've spoken to me first."

"Would you have been more open then?" he countered. "If I spoke to you about it first? Be honest."

His voice rumbled through the room, low, still soft, but still carrying weight.

All Rylee did was sigh.

"Exactly," he whispered.

Rylee pressed her head even firmer to his chest, her hand wrapping tighter around him, which made him fight his smile... giving in, even though he didn't want to.

"I love you, baby," she said against him, pressing a kiss to his shoulder. Then another.

Xander closed his eyes at the feel of her hand smoothing up to his face then her teasing him by brushing her lips against the maze of his ear. Rylee turned his jaw so he could look at her in the dark. Then she leaned in and pressed a kiss to his lips.

He moaned. Folding like a paper plane.

Damn.

Xander was so easy when it came to Rylee.

And he knew it.

He didn't hesitate to turn to face her, pulling her even closer. Her baby bump between them did the job of touching his heart, reminding him that despite her want to hang on to the past, their future was here... and so close... something she wouldn't be able to deny for much longer.

But he left it for the night. Unresolved.

Because something in him always gave way whenever she touched him like that. That thread of intimacy between them stayed alive, tethering them even in disagreement.

So as he kissed her back, moving her into position to make love, Xander knew... as much as Rylee wanted that to be the first and last conversation about the house... it couldn't be.

He pressed kisses onto her, let her think it was over.

But in the quiet of the dark, Xander knew this couldn't be the last time they talked about the house. Not because he wanted to win, but because their lives were growing... whether they were ready or not.

Still, for now, he let it rest.

She needed time.

And he could wait.

## RYLEE

LAUGHTER TRAVELED AROUND THE TABLE, bouncing off the ceilings and walls of the restaurant.

Seated at a long table that stretched from one end of the room to the other sat Rylee, Xander, and all the people they loved.

They were in a softly lit, upscale restaurant in Brooklyn, a mile from the brownstone.

Floor-to-ceiling windows gave views of the city street at night. Traffic lights lit up. Passersby peeked in. And Rylee basked in the intimate ambiance of the evening.

Xander had reserved the biggest table in the restaurant for the night for their baby shower. A very lowkey, last minute affair.

He placed a hand on her stomach as he leaned in, his other arm already around her shoulder. "You good?"

She nodded.

She was more than good. Surrounded by everyone she loved—including her parents, Lennox's parents, her girlfriends, children, and Xander's mother, their extended family, and his firefighter crew—how could she be anything but good?

Nova and LJ sat to Rylee's left, between her and her mother, who was cutting a piece of the chocolate cake that remained on LJ's plate to feed him.

The baby shower was the most laidback setup one could have ever seen.

There were no blue balloons. No shower games on the table.

This was for the grown. Just how Rylee and Xander wanted it.

In his free hand was a cigar, courtesy of Rylee's dad, Gannon.

"So, you guys have everything set up, right?" Xander's friend, Jamal, asked. He sat beside Xander's mother, who was seated beside Xander. Jamal gestured toward his wife who sat to his left. "If I remember anything from our kids, it's best to have all that stuff set up to be prepared for any and all surprises."

"*Been* had those things set up." Xander peeked over at Rylee and winked.

"Xander insisted," Rylee added with a smile. "For the biggest event of the year, he's been preparing for it from before we knew what we were having."

"Well, it won't be the *only* biggest event, ain't that right, Xander?" Gannon chuckled from the other side of the table beside Lennox's parents, The Walkers, who insisted on being present for every major milestone... including this one.

Xander scratched the back of his neck and shot a look across the table at Gannon, who quickly folded his lips into his mouth to laugh to himself.

Rylee looked between the two, noticing their silent exchange— her internal voice flagging what just happened, something that seemingly went unnoticed by everyone else at the table.

"Well, Xander knows *all* about those surprises," Xander's chief confirmed from down the table. "He's had to deliver quite a few babies during his EMT years."

"Oh yes," Xander's mother, Michelle, chimed in, wrapping her arm around his shoulder. "I've heard a few of those stories."

Rylee peeked over at him, and he looked to her.

"Regular ol' Superman, huh?" she teased between them.

Xander popped his collar and placed his cigar in his mouth, making Rylee giggle. "Superman ain't got nothing on me, baby."

She laughed this time.

The night felt good. Surrounded by family and friends, conversation easily flowing from one topic to the next. It was everything Rylee imagined it being and then some.

"All right," one of the servers who had been catering the group announced as she approached. "I'll place this here."

She set the black book—with the bill tucked inside—on the table between Xander and Rylee.

"Whenever you're ready," the server added.

"Oh, we're ready," Xander said, prepared to push his chair back and pull out his wallet.

"Oh no, Claudia and I got it, Xander," Gannon said across the table, hand outstretched for the book.

"No, no, no," Lennox's father, Mr. Walker, voiced, waving a hand in the air and beckoning for the black book a second later. "Ivy and I can take care of it."

"*Aw*, y'all are too sweet," Michelle was next to speak over them all, reaching for the book. "I've got it."

"There's no way the department is going to let anyone pay for tonight's meal." Chief Logan pushed his seat back. "Just send it down this way, Cox."

Rylee scoffed a laugh. "You guys, please," she said, picking up the book. "We got it."

"Rylee, don't you touch that book," Michelle warned, tapping Xander. "Baby, give it to me."

"Nope!" Parker, Rylee's friend, shouted from down the table. "Send it here. Nadia and I already said—"

"*I* am paying," Gannon said over everyone. "And *that* is final."

By that point, debating ensued, everyone stating why they should settle the bill. All of them on their feet except Rylee, Xander, and the giggling kids who found humor in the exchanges.

Rylee peeked up at the server. "I'm so sorry."

"Oh no, *please*." The server giggled, pressing a hand to her chest. "What a beautiful problem to have. We usually see the opposite."

Xander laughed.

The server smiled. "You guys take your time figuring it out. I'll be back."

Over the voices that traveled around the table—everyone stating why they'd take care of it—Rylee locked eyes with Xander.

He leaned in and kissed her softly before rubbing his nose with hers, making her giggle.

"What a beautiful problem to have, for real."

"To be so loved by stubborn people." Rylee leaned her head on his shoulder.

Xander's hand moved to her stomach to rub as they listened to everyone around them. "Definitely."

Rylee's chest swelled with gratitude as she listened to everyone playfully arguing, wondering... could the night get any better than this?

* * *

"The fact that they split that bill all them ways just so they could all pay," Rylee said as she shut off the water in the bathroom. "These people."

Xander laughed from inside of the bedroom.

She chuckled, reaching forward to pick up one of the folded face towels on her vanity.

Rylee felt a slight ache in her lower back and pressed a hand there while stretching back and sighing.

Before she could feel the dull pain for too long, Xander was right there, pressing a hand to the area, gently massaging it.

"Thank you." She smiled. "He's getting heavy."

"I seen this thing online," Xander told her, moving in closer behind her. "Let me know if this helps."

Xander grabbed her belly from its underside and gently lifted it, slowly, balancing the weight of it in his hands.

Rylee gasped at the sudden wave of relief that washed over her. The comfort of feeling several pounds lighter was instant and overwhelming. Her head fell back as the weight lifted—off her body and off her shoulders—giving her a glimpse of the relief she hoped to feel once she gave birth.

She was in the last day of her eighth month and this was around the time she started to feel fed up with being pregnant. This pregnancy had been the easiest of them all, though, as Xander promised.

Mostly because if he heard a complaint or heard Rylee express a craving, he was right on it.

Like right now, holding her belly up carefully so she could experience the bliss of weightlessness only for a few breaths.

"Oh, I love you *so* much," she whispered and he snickered behind her, pressing a kiss to her cheek.

"Go ahead and lay down," he directed, gently releasing his hold on her belly. "I'll be there in a moment to get back to rubbing your back."

She moaned. "I am so spoiled and I love that for me."

He kissed the top of her head and Rylee turned to leave the bathroom as advised.

She made her way to her side of the bed, still beaming from the day. Rylee really enjoyed herself at their baby shower. It was unconventional but dressed in *so* much love, she was still buzzing from the energy.

She'd gotten to her side of the bed, pulled back the covers, and blinked hard when she spotted a diamond ring on her pillow.

The black velvet box that held the diamond in its slit was small, but not the ring. The ring's diamond was prominent, and glowing under the lamplight on her side table.

The stone caught the light at every angle, causing Rylee to completely freeze in place.

She turned to the bathroom, doing her best to find the words to ask Xander about it, when she found him down on one knee inches away from her.

That made her gasp then press her hand to her chest.

Xander was silent for a beat before he chuckled nervously. "I'm scared as *hell* right now."

Rylee released a small laugh that was all breath.

Instantly, she remembered her father's comment during dinner and the look him and Xander exchanged in that moment.

"I'm terrified," Xander continued, "Not because I don't want to marry you, because, *God*, I really do. And I'm not terrified because I don't think I'll be a great husband or father, because I know for damn sure I will be."

Her heart was pounding now.

"I'm scared you won't let me show you any of that, Snoop."

Rylee's eyes were blinking so quickly now, tears forming as she kept them on Xander.

There he was, all six-foot-something of him. Arms bulging, shoulders squared. Just a whole lot of man, on one knee... for her.

"Three years ago, this life I'm living now with you was the furthest thing from my desires," Xander confessed. "I wasn't thinking wife, kids, house... a house she won't accept." He shook his head then licked his lips. "But then I saw you... snooping through my mother's trash—"

"Aye," Rylee cut in, pointing at him. "I was not snooping through nobody's trash."

He smirked. "Yeah, you were."

Rylee rolled her eyes and tried to fight back her smile but lost.

"And it was the greatest discovery of my life, Rylee," he said, waiting for her attention again. "Because you entered my life with not just your amazing self but with absolutely awesome children who stole my heart just as quickly as you did mine." He sniffed back his tears. "So for real, Rylee? I'm not asking you to marry me."

Rylee's brows wrinkled.

"Because that would be too easy, too cliché," he added, pressing his hand to his chest. "I'm asking you to let me love you the way you deserve. To show you how amazing of a husband I can be to you because... you're the love of my life. And it's like I said, I understand Lennox will always be a part of you. But you're my future, and though I've never met him, I think he'd like that for you... at least I'd hope he would."

She smiled, the tears pooling more now in her eyes.

"And I think he'd like me for you too." He nodded. "I know that shit. 'Cause I'm me."

She laughed softly this time.

"And because I love you so much, Rylee." Xander extended a hand to her and Rylee closed the distance between them.

Once her hand was in his, Xander asked, "So, will you allow me a chance to do that? Will you be my wife, Rylee... please?"

Her bottom lip quivered at the sight of him and at his words. The gentle caress of his thumb over the back of her hand and the soft look in his eyes.

Her hand went to her belly and his hand covered hers on top of it.

And even though her heart was racing, her mind moving even faster with how much things had changed in just a few months, the only answer she wanted to say came out of her mouth with ease. So much ease.

"Yes," she said, softly and with tears. "I absolutely will. *Yes!*"

The smile on Xander's face could've lit the Manhattan skyline.

He rose from his knee and pulled her to him. Pressed a kiss so deep against her lips, Rylee went warm all over in his embrace and wrapped her arms as far around him as she could manage.

A moment later, Xander broke their kiss to retrieve the ring, plucking it from the box and sliding it onto her finger.

"Thank you," he said to her, pulling her close.

"Thank *you*." Rylee pressed her head to him, closing her eyes, a tear escaping once more. "Because you're already making me the happiest woman in the galaxy."

Xander tightened his arm around her then kissed the top of her braids. "And I'm just getting warmed up."

Rylee laughed again, hugging him tighter.

Earlier she wondered could the night get better.

And it did.

# *sixteen*

## RYLEE

"THANKS SO MUCH FOR STAYING, LIZ," Rylee said, walking to one of the available chairs in the basement.

"Of course," Liz replied with a short laugh.

Rylee waddled the rest of the way to her seat, sighing the moment she was able to sit and relax.

"Later, you two," Ivy Pressman, the final group member said, waving as she exited the basement.

"Bye, Ivy," Rylee said from her seat, waving back. "Give Levi a huge kiss for me when you get home."

"And will." Ivy giggled, her voice fading as she left the basement.

It was the day of Rylee's group meeting. This was one of the rare ones where Rylee's therapist, Liz Peters, visited to sit in on discussions, offer advice, tips, and assignments to the group members to assist with their healing from loss.

The Hope Collective was truly one of Rylee's pride and joys. She was doing everything she could to put things in order in time for her maternity leave.

With that thought, her hand rested on her belly. The moment her fingertips pressed into the roundest part of her stomach, the baby moved, making her scoff a laugh.

"I literally can't even rest my hand here without him wanting to play in there," she commented, shaking her head. "I can only imagine how he'll be when he gets here. Probably a lot like his father."

The sun was setting in Brooklyn. But Rylee couldn't tell, being in the windowless basement of the bookstore where she hosted her meetings.

Liz smiled across from Rylee, crossing her legs in her seat, then leaning her face into her hand that was held up by her elbow resting on the chair's armrest where she sat. "You glow so much when you're pregnant."

Rylee's cheeks warmed. "Do I?"

"*Mmm-hmm.*" Liz nodded then used her pen to point at Rylee's hand. "But that ring is giving you some competition, Rylee. I can't even lie."

Rylee laughed.

"Still getting used to seeing it there." Rylee extended her hand to admire her ring.

Liz smirked. "Well, I might need to wear sunglasses the next time we meet."

"Oh, *please*," Rylee said through her laugh.

Liz's smile grew, her eyes seeming to water as she allowed her smile to rest on her lips. "I'm *so* proud of you."

Rylee inhaled a deep breath then pressed her hand to her chest.

"When we first met, never would I have imagined *this*." Liz pressed her hands to her chest. "Then after you lost Lennox, I knew I had my work cut out for me because you'd become guarded, grief-stricken... understandably. But now..."

"I know," Rylee whispered, closing her eyes. "I can't believe it some mornings either. Like, how did I get here?"

"With work," Liz answered. "And a commitment... to yourself. To your healing. Most importantly, patience and not giving up on your-self. *That's* how."

"Yeah." Rylee blinked back tears.

She knew what Liz was saying was true. But Rylee also knew she wasn't completely changed… and that she was still carrying whatever element inside herself that made her resistant to sudden changes.

"Well," Rylee started, taking another big inhale of the air around them. She picked up traces of old books stacked on the shelves in the basement before releasing the air on an exhale. "I can admit I've grown but I'm *still* hardheaded, Liz."

Liz arched a brow.

"Change still feels threatening sometimes… even when I *know* the change is good, you know?"

Liz reached for her trusty black book and Rylee grinned to herself. What she wouldn't give to get a little peek inside that thing.

As soon as Liz flipped the book open and pressed down on her pen's ejector, she looked up at Rylee and asked, "What's going on?"

Rylee spent the next few minutes telling Liz all about the house in Greene Gardens Xander bought without telling her. She also shared how him buying the house, although he meant well, triggered fears inside of her she hadn't yet addressed and didn't really want to either.

"You know Ivy Pressman, right?" Rylee asked. "The woman who just left here?"

"*Mmm-hmm,*" Liz replied.

"She lives out there. In Greene Gardens," Rylee explained. "She says it's amazing, and perfect for her and her little family. But… it's *not* the brownstone here in Brooklyn."

Liz tilted her head to one side.

Rylee planted her Jordans on the floor and used her leverage to push herself up in her chair.

"Lennox bought that brownstone for us," she explained. "He wanted to raise Nova under one roof and bought it so that we could do that. Granted, we didn't account for having another baby, but still, I made room… moved into Lennox's bedroom after he died and gave Nova mine, and gave Nova's old room to LJ. But now…" She sighed. "I know Xander is right. We're going to need more space. But my whole life is in that brownstone, Liz. I've made a home there, and…"

Liz sat silently, waiting.

Rylee shook her head, knowing what she wanted to say but not wanting to put it out there… knowing she'd need to address it. Liz wouldn't have it any other way.

"Say it, Rylee," Liz encouraged, seeming to read Ryle's mind. "Say the thing you want to say."

Rylee squeezed her eyes closed then sucked her teeth. "It's the last piece of Lennox I have and I don't want to let it go."

Liz nodded slowly, lowering her attention to her black book to jot something down.

"If the brownstone is gone, that's it," Rylee continued. "I would have completely removed him from my life. The children could possibly forget him, since Nova's early memories of her father are literally planted in the walls of that brownstone."

Rylee bit at her bottom lip.

"The brownstone is *more* than *just* a brownstone to me. It's stability. It's family. It's our home. And leaving it… I'm just *so scared* of what leaving might symbolize."

"These are all valid feelings, Rylee." Liz nodded. "I want to start there."

Rylee released the air she didn't realize she was holding onto.

"What you are feeling is real. What you are fearing is understandable," Liz added. "Keeping yourself in this state of fear and worry is *not*."

Liz uncrossed her legs and moved to the edge of her seat.

"Change is unsettling, but it is the only constant in life. You say the brownstone means all these things to you, but it isn't the brownstone that's holding those things. *You* are."

Rylee blinked in response.

"That brownstone can go tomorrow. It can be reduced to rubble and ash, but the memories and what you've created there won't. The physical stuff, yes. But the feeling? That's all you. You can take that *anywhere*... even to this house in Greene Gardens."

Rylee looked off, digesting Liz's words. As always, her words always sounded doable until Rylee had to actually do them.

"Have you seen the house in Greene Gardens?"

Rylee nodded. "Yeah, in pictures."

"No," Liz said with a shake of her head. "Have you actually seen the house? Gone to Greene Gardens to step foot inside to see what Xander sees?"

"Well... *no*."

Liz sat silently, waiting for Rylee to continue.

"To be real, Liz," Rylee continued. "We haven't spoken about the house since he brought it up. My reaction was so sudden and unyielding, which is probably why he hasn't brought it up again... *that* and because I said that was our first and last conversation about it."

Liz's eyes were on her book again when she advised, "You should at least see the house, Rylee. In person."

Rylee twisted her lips to one side, listening.

"Not because you're going to say yes to moving there. Because you have every right to say no," Liz added, lifting her gaze to Rylee. "But you should see it after the baby is born. You'll have a new beginning you can't deny in your arms when you go to see the house. And going will be a courageous step forward."

Rylee's eyes darted between Liz's.

"Because as much as you may not want it, change is going to happen." She smiled. "And it's better to be an ally to change instead of being an enemy of it. That's where the struggle happens. Opposition where one need not exist. And with something so beautiful and a gesture from Xander so pure and forward-thinking, the least you can do is go and see what *he* sees."

Rylee nodded thoughtfully, her hand back to rubbing her stomach, her son back to rolling around in response to her touch.

"You're right. And I hate it when you're right sometimes."

Liz giggled.

Rylee lowered her attention to her left hand on her stomach. Her diamond winked at the lights above, making her smile. But it wasn't the ring that drew the smile. It was Xander's words before he put the ring there. They were stuck in her memory. Not in an annoying way, but stuck like a gentle reminder she wanted to remain pinned in place. His asking her to let him show her he could love her the way she needed to be loved. That mattered.

The least she could do was allow that. And one way would be to see the house. At least.

"Okay," Rylee voiced, refocused her eyes on Liz again. "I'll go. After the baby is born. One step at a time, right?"

"Exactly." Liz grinned. "And Rylee, remember, you're healing... and you will continue to do so. Everything you do should be to facilitate that, even when it's scary."

Rylee nodded.

"Healing doesn't mean forgetting," Liz reminded, leaning forward to press a hand to Rylee's knee. "It means making space for more life."

"Right," Rylee said low. "You're so right."

* * *

"Aight." Xander held the door open for Rylee to walk through. "I think we've bought enough of the store for the day."

Rylee chuckled as she waddled past him, one hand holding a bag, the other pressing to her back.

A Braxton Hicks contraction held her stomach in a firm grip, releasing its hold as quickly as it arrived.

Her due date was officially in one week, and she was starting to feel the weight of it all. Rylee's mother was convinced the baby would be here before the due date, because according to her, Rylee's stomach had dropped.

But Rylee insisted her mother was wrong yet again.

*"You said that for both of your grandchildren," Rylee argued as she sat in her mother's chair while her mother installed a new set of braids in Rylee's hair. "You said that with Nova, and she came after her due date. Said the same thing about LJ, and he did the same. My stomach dropping really means nothing, Mama."*

*"Mmm-hmm, whatever." Her mother adjusted Rylee's head. "Just keep your head still so I can finish these braids. The last thing we need is you going into labor with a half-finished head."*

That was three days ago, and still no signs of labor for Rylee. Braxton Hicks had just started to happen here and there—like as Rylee stood in one of the aisles in the baby store that evening and as she and Xander made their way to the car—but nothing she wasn't used to, nothing any different than with LJ or Nova.

"Let me get that bag, Snoop," Xander insisted, taking quick steps toward Rylee. "Over here struggling."

"Struggling?" Rylee laughed. "This bag has baby towels, Xander. Stop it."

"Don't matter," Xander said, reaching for the bag. "There's a lot of baby towels in there. Too many."

"Trust me," Rylee debated. "There is no such thing as too many baby towels. You'll see."

*"Mmm-hmm,"* Xander replied. He curled his fingers around the bag's handles and stepped in front of her, stopping her with the toe of his sneaker just nudging hers. "Give it to me."

The two had intentionally matched sneakers—Xander's idea. Whenever they went out to run errands or to hang out just them two, he insisted they wear the same footwear or matching colors.

It was his thing.

And Rylee thought it to be so cute.

For their errand that day, they stopped by a baby store in Brooklyn to pick up some last-minute things. Pacifiers, baby towels, swaddling blankets, and socks. Things they didn't put on their gift registry—a registry that had been cleared out by their friends and family.

"What you thinking about for food?" Xander asked, taking Rylee's hand as they walked through the parking lot, headed for his truck. The truck was the most spacious of their vehicles, and as Rylee got bigger in pregnancy, she favored room and either insisted she take his truck or he drive her in it.

"Tacos?" he asked next, as they neared his truck. "We can pick some up, take it back to the house?"

Rylee's deep dish dimples appeared, highlighting her smile.

"Since the kids are at their grandparents, we can eat them with nothing on in the kitchen," Xander added, briefly sticking his tongue out. "You know, the way tacos are supposed to be enjoyed."

Rylee hollered a laugh. "You silly."

The mention of the kids being away and them having the brownstone all to themselves made her recall the conversation she had with Liz a few weeks prior. The conversation about the house in Greene Gardens. A house Xander had not brought up since showing her a picture of it.

As Xander opened the door, Rylee was struck with a sudden impulsive feeling she was shocked to be feeling in that moment.

But they were alone, it was still a little early in the evening... so why not?

"Can we go somewhere else before we get the tacos?"

Xander held his hand out for her to take so he could help her step up and into the truck. "Sure. Where you tryna go?"

"The house," she answered. "In Greene Gardens."

He jerked his head back so hard it could have fallen off if he didn't have a neck holding it up.

"Here," she said, smiling. "Close the door and get inside."

She didn't have to tell Xander twice. He wore his confusion from the time he closed her door to his walk around the truck to get into his seat on the driver's side.

The moment he closed the door, and as he placed their shopping bags in the back seat, Rylee turned to face him.

"You came up in my therapy session a few weeks back."

Xander held her attention but said nothing.

"And… so did the house," she added. "And Liz suggested I take a trip out there to see what you see."

"Okay…"

"I was going to wait until after the baby arrived, but we don't have the kids here and you said it's not that far from Brooklyn, right?"

"Not too far at all," he answered, nodding. "Right."

Though he was doing everything to keep his cool, Rylee could see the cautious excitement on his face. She could hear it in his tone too. His voice was deeper, words slower to leave his mouth—which was so not Xander.

It melted her heart seeing him try to be composed when he clearly wanted to be excited.

That made it all the more important for them to go right then and there.

So at Rylee's insistence, they took off in the direction of Greene Gardens.

As they drove, Xander's awe was palpable. He couldn't keep to himself how excited he was for Rylee to see the place as they got closer.

The ride was smooth, no traffic. It was the other side of the expressway that was bumper to bumper, with only the shoulders of the road clear for the most part.

Everything looked pretty much the same through the windshield to Rylee… until Xander drove past the village's entrance sign.

*Welcome to Greene Gardens.*

The logo looked official, and from a distance, lights could be seen glowing.

A mile from the sign and after crossing a small bridge that led into the village, Rylee blinked hard at how alive it looked.

"Wow," she expressed with more air than tone.

She peeked over at Xander, who smiled and nodded.

"I know," he voiced, just as in awe.

For a village that had just undergone construction a few years back, the way people filled the streets and the number of shops that were open for patrons... you'd think the village had been there for years.

Rylee's eyes were glued to her passenger window as she caught sight of families outside, enjoying the autumn night. Shops were bustling, music playing from some.

Rylee pressed her hand to her chest, her eyes trying to keep up with the truck's movement and the people.

Black people of all shades filled the streets and sidewalks. It was like a scene out of a Black film.

Streets were clean. Lights shined bright.

It looked like Brooklyn—except cleaner, quainter, and with fresher air.

"I was *not* expecting *this*," Rylee said as they turned down a block that quickly became residential.

"Neither was I when I first visited," Xander said in response.

There were homes lining both sides of the tree-lined blocks. Expensive cars were either parked on the curb or in driveways.

Rylee's eyes moved with those trees, unblinking. "I gotta give Bryant a call tomorrow and get some answers, because damn."

Xander chuckled.

"This is amazing," Rylee whispered. "How does someone imagine this? Wow.

Her eyes locked in on a familiar property. One she'd only seen in a picture on Xander's phone. The one she thought was beautiful.

But in person, there was no comparison.

It looked huge in the photo, but as they pulled up in front of it... it was colossal.

A colossal structure of beauty, from the roof to the manicured lawn.

She refused to let go of her breath as Xander opened the door to step out.

The block was quiet. The homes in the area were all complete, lights on in some, off in others... including the one they'd pulled up in front of.

The architectural details of the house were stunning. It was like they took their time with this one. Large, crystal-clear windows that offered a beautiful view inside.

She wasn't sure what it was, but the second Xander helped her out of his truck and they took the small steps up to the front door... the feeling of apprehension, worry, fear... it wasn't there.

Instead, those feelings were replaced with safety. Comfort. A sudden openness... for the future.

"Aight," Xander said after turning the key in the front door and opening it. "Come on in."

As Rylee's Jordans created thuds along the hardwood flooring that echoed around them in the empty space, Xander explained the vision for every room.

The living room was bigger than the living room in the brownstone. Space for a dining room, and even more space for something else.

The stairs were winding. Beautifully structured. Sturdy.

The backyard gave way to an immense amount of land, perfect for events that could fit at least fifty of their closest friends and family.

And when he helped her up the stairs to the bedrooms, she felt her eyes prick with tears.

She could hear Nova and LJ squealing at how much space each room had. LJ always felt a way that Nova's room was bigger than his. That argument wouldn't even be a thing anymore.

"It's perfect," she commented as they stood in the middle of the master bedroom. There were skylights in the en suite and in the room, windows with a view of the area of the house.

"*Okay*. I can see us here."

Those words were more for her than Xander, honestly. She said them low but loud enough to be heard. Loud enough for it to resonate with something inside of her that aided in warming to the idea of this being more than just a visit.

"I've never built anything of my own," he admitted quietly behind her. "Not a home, not a family. I just wanted... *something* to offer you that feels solid. And you know... *this* feels solid, Snoop."

She turned to look at Xander. He towered in the room.

The high ceilings accommodated his stature. So did the front door. So did the trek up the stairs.

Everything was perfect. Not just for her and the kids... but him too.

Rylee parted her lips to say all of that. To say that he'd done good—finding something for himself and for their family—but stopped when she felt the baby roll, then kick.

And suddenly... she heard a pop.

Her hand flew to her stomach.

Xander's smile fell instantly as her eyes locked on his, her brows in a furrow.

He bent his legs at the knees to meet her eyes. "What's up?"

The seat of her panties gradually warmed, and a second later, a gush of water sloshed out of her, soaking her black sweatpants instantly.

Xander's eyes grew so wide. "Oh. Shit."

"Oh, my God." Rylee peeked down at the puddle of water around her wet sneakers. "Oh, my God, my mother was right!"

Indeed she was... because Rylee's water had just broken.

"What?" Xander asked, taking her hand.

"We have to go," she said instead. "Right *now*."

Without another word, Xander took Rylee's hand, helping her down the stairs, out of the house, and into the truck.

The calm driving they were doing away from the house became much faster, Xander doing just above the speed limit as they drove past the Greene Gardens welcome sign.

The bumps in their ride sent a wave of sensations through Rylee.

"Just breathe, baby," Xander coached, his eyes volleying between the road and his fiancée. "Shit, we don't have the overnight bag you packed."

"My mother told me," Rylee said, feeling her stomach tighten with a contraction. "She fucking told me."

Xander reached across to her, placing a hand on her belly for comfort.

He snatched his eyes off the road immediately, his hand feeling around her stomach. "It's hard. Are you having a contraction?"

She peeked down, then up at him again. "A Braxton, maybe."

He felt again, shaking his head. "This don't feel like a Braxton, baby. You not feeling anything stronger right now?"

She shook her head. "How would you know the difference just feeling my stomach?"

"Experience," he mumbled, anxiety evident in the wrinkle of his brows and the biting he was doing on his bottom lip.

In his haste and distracted in conversation while simply getting on the expressway to get to the birthing center in Brooklyn, Xander missed the pothole they were approaching and only noticed it as they were going over it.

The impact rattled the truck, shaking them in their seats, and triggering a strong contraction Rylee most definitely felt this time.

She shouted.

"Fuck," he exhaled. "Sorry. You okay?"

That one contraction rolled immediately into another... and then another.

"Oh, God!" she gasped, pressing one hand to her stomach and the other to the handle on the door. "*Ahh!* Shit."

"It's aight, it's aight," Xander repeated.

He stopped speaking altogether as the truck gradually began to reduce in speed.

Rylee opened her eyes to a sea of red taillights in front of her.

"Oh, no," she said, her head falling back against the headrest.

The traffic jam they'd passed on the way to the house in Greene Gardens that seemed unfortunate on the other side of the expressway was now what they found themselves stopped in.

"Okay," Xander said, rubbing her belly, his other hand gripping the steering wheel as he moved the truck up in the slow-moving traffic. "You got this, baby. Just breathe with me."

That worked for the first fifteen minutes... then the half an hour of sitting in traffic.

As much progress as they had made in traffic, the exit to the birthing center was still only 1.2 miles away. The contractions were back to back now, and Rylee was panicking.

Then suddenly, she felt the pressure between her thighs. And while her pregnancies before this one were different all the way around, that feeling was familiar.

Her moaning and groaning quickly transformed into screaming.

"I feel like I gotta push!" she shouted.

Rylee felt the air move as Xander looked her way.

"I don't know why I feel like I have to push," she cried. "But I have to push, Xander."

She tried to hold it in, but her body was not trying to cooperate.

Her face misted with sweat as another contraction rolled through. She tried to close her legs... but the urge to push gripped every muscle in her body like a vice, leaving her no choice but to give in.

She screamed as the wave of her contraction built and reached a high, and she bared down uncontrollably.

"Okay, okay." Xander switched on his hazard lights and honked as he moved the truck up and over to the shoulder of the road. "I got you. I'm pulling over."

"What is happening?" Rylee cried out, her face now wet with tears. "It's too soon. My water just broke."

"Precipitous labor," Xander said, his voice steady, calmer. "You're in active labor now. Dr. Grayson warned us about this."

Rylee's heart felt like it was in her throat as she felt another contraction creeping up.

"This is your third child." Xander put the car in park and unhooked his seatbelt. "Labor likely already started while we were shopping. Open your door, Rylee."

Rylee did as told. Her body was shaking, hands trembling... something she only noticed when she was opening the door.

"Aight," Xander said outside, peeling off his hoodie by the sleeves. The breeze from outside whipped against her face, cooling her.

He was grabbing her by her legs when he told her, "Can you turn toward me, baby? Yeah, just like that."

Rylee did as told, barely able to move but doing it anyway. "Xander—"

"Sit sideways," he coached over her. "One leg on the seat."

Her breaths were coming in faster than she could stop them, but still, she carried out his request.

"Yeah." He nodded, eyes firmly on her as he removed her sneakers. "Now put the other up on the dash if you can."

"Xander, what's happening?" she asked, doing as told.

"That's it." He exhaled slowly through his mouth, forcing a smile while nodding. "Stick right here, I'll be right back."

Her heart was pounding now. The sounds of honking cars, passing winds, and the natural sounds of the expressway they traveled down cluttered her sound space.

Another contraction rolled through her and she gritted her teeth while trying to hold back her scream and the sensation to push, but she struggled to do both.

She watched Xander open the backseat of his truck to retrieve something, then head to the trunk and grab a bottle of isopropyl alcohol. He poured it over his hands, the sharp scent instantly rising into the cold air.

"Aight," he said as he returned in front of her, pushing air through his mouth. He grabbed at the waistband of her sweatpants and her heart dropped.

"Xander, what the fuck?!"

He looked up at her, and she held his gaze.

"I'm scared," she admitted, her bottom lip trembling. "This can't happen. I can't have him right now. I don't want something to happen to him—"

"Look at me." Xander crouched down on the ground outside, his breath still steady, his warm hand holding her by the side of her face. "You got me, and I got you. And we've got him," he said, placing his hand on her hard belly. "You are *not* alone, and you don't have to be scared. Aight?"

With her pants off, Xander got low to check, using his fingers to measure how far she'd dilated.

He looked up at her, eyes focused. "Baby... you're fully dilated."

"Oh, God."

Xander slid his hoodie underneath her next and grabbed one of the towels he got from the backseat.

His eyes returned to hers when he told her, "With your next contraction I need you to push just like you were doing, okay?"

And just as he was instructing, another contraction rolled through, holding Rylee tight around her belly and sending a wave of pain throughout her.

Rylee bared down and pushed, screaming through the whole thing and only having enough energy to catch her breath and do it again. Not that she had a choice. Her body was pushing her to do only that... push.

"Good, baby," he said, his voice a little higher. "You're doing incredible. Just breathe. Big breath in and blow it out."

She did and pushed again when her body signaled her to. Her hand gripped the headrest as she bared her teeth, feeling like she'd shatter them but committing to being okay with that if it meant getting her and their son through this in one piece.

It was in her next push that she felt the sting that always felt like it would rip her in half. The ring of fire stretch she'd felt when Nova and LJ's heads were right there.

"Oh my *God!*" She screamed. "His head."

"I know, baby," Xander shouted back. "I know. You got this—"

"He's coming," she said over him. "I can feel him—"

"Yeah, he's coming," Xander said, peeking down between her legs, his voice catching. "I see him, Snoop. He's right there, baby."

His voice was heavy in emotion but still guidance, and somehow, that gave Rylee more comfort than panic in the moment.

Another contraction built from the base of her spine, traveling up her stomach and seeming like it was holding her by her throat.

"One more push, Rylee," Xander coached. "Give me one more *big* push."

Rylee bared down with a scream, this one straining her vocal cords. It was mixed in with crying and sobbing, but still, determination. Her voice echoed around them as her body tensed. Her hand flew to the dashboard to brace herself.

"Okay… okay…" Xander shouted, voice breaking, his hands steady. "I got his head. I got it in my hand. The cord's not around his neck, so you're good, baby. You're good. Give me one more, Rylee. One more, mama."

Rylee screamed and pushed as hard as she could this time, holding the position and her breath. The moment she felt tiny limbs move out of her, she dropped back against the truck's center console behind herself, chest rising, breaths heavy.

There was silence… until the baby's cries pierced the moment.

And the cry made Rylee exhale all the air inside of her.

"Oh, God," she heard Xander express, his voice heavy in emotion as the baby's cry challenged any sound around them. "You did it, baby. You did it."

Rylee's head was spinning, her eyes heavy. She felt lightheaded but ignored it. And it was easy to, with the adrenaline pulsing through her veins, her mind on a natural, intense high.

A chill washed over her, starting at her toes and slowly traveling up her legs.

"Rylee?"

Xander's voice sounded distant, more like an echo than his actual tone. He suddenly seemed so far away, even though he was standing right in front of her.

She couldn't move. Couldn't open her eyes either.

"Rylee?!" Xander shouted in a panic.

She felt him lift her head but she had no energy to hold it up herself. Her vision blurred, her hands trembling, the sweat on her lip now cold.

"Oh, God, Rylee, stay with me," Xander said in a panic, his voice echoing even more. "Open your eyes, baby. Look at me, Rylee."

She couldn't.

Warmth seemed to pour out beneath her, but she couldn't tell what it was.

"Shit," Xander hissed low, almost to himself. "Shit. Shit. Shit! The placenta hasn't even detached yet and there's blood everywhere. You're bleeding out. Fuck."

Rylee sensed movement over her.

"Stay with me, Rylee," Xander said in one breath. "Stay with me."

She couldn't understand why her mouth wouldn't form the words.

She wanted to say she was tired. That she'd just get some sleep… just for a little while. But her lips felt sealed shut by something outside of her control.

"This is Firefighter Cox, badge 241," Xander shouted into what she could only assume was his phone. "I need an ambulance on the BQE westbound, near exit 29. Emergency roadside delivery. We've got blood loss and the mother is losing consciousness. *Please*. Hurry!"

The last thing Rylee felt was Xander's cold hand at the side of her face.

The baby continued to cry beneath Xander's voice, but Rylee no longer had the strength to respond. All she could do was drift.

"No," Xander stuttered. "Rylee, you stay with me. You hear me? You don't get to leave, baby. Not now. Not after this."

She could hear her heart beating in her ears, but even that sound was fading.

"We just started," she heard in the distance. "You hear me? We just started."

And a heartbeat later... everything went dark.

seventeen

XANDER

XANDER FELT himself nodding off but quickly came to, the soft beeping of the heart monitor doing just enough to keep him awake.

The hospital room was dimly lit. Brooklyn's city lights shimmered beyond the window, casting a faint glow.

He looked down at the quiet, warm weight in his arms.

His son.

Even through his haze of exhaustion, Xander couldn't help but smile.

The last five hours had been the most traumatic of his life. That was saying a lot, considering his history as a former EMT and current firefighter.

Xander had never been so grateful for the life he'd lived. The calls he'd answered. The hours he'd worked. His years in ambulances.

Now in his thirties, all those lives led him here.

Because although he'd delivered babies before—during emergency calls, in the back of ambulances—he never thought he'd ever deliver his *own* child... on the side of the road... in his truck.

His eyes moved off the baby and onto Rylee.

Still sound asleep in the hospital bed.

A real-life sleeping beauty.

She didn't look anything like what she'd just endured.

She looked serene. Beautiful, of course. But more than that, she looked at peace.

Xander inhaled deeply, pressing his free hand to the corner of his eye, trying to stay present.

It had to be after three a.m., maybe closer to four.

The doctors told him he could go home and rest. They'd call when Rylee woke up.

They said she'd likely sleep through the night, especially after all the medication they'd given her once he got her there.

Just the thought of that made his heart hammer.

Because God... things could have gone very differently.

He looked back down at his son.

His junior.

Just a month ago, he and Rylee had decided to name the baby after him. Xander had been all for it.

He could've gone back to the brownstone, gotten a few hours of rest. But his soon-to-be wife and his son were here.

So this was where he needed to be.

He kept his eyes on Rylee's chest, watching it rise and fall. The steady rhythm anchored him.

He'd counted it at least a thousand times. Checked her pulse just as many.

He was ready to check it again in another few minutes.

The baby stirred in his arms just as he heard another stir to his right.

Xander turned his head, locking eyes on Rylee, watching her slowly blink awake.

He sat up straight, stopping himself from standing too fast when he remembered he still had their son in his arms.

Carefully, he rose and walked the baby to the bassinet just a step away.

Behind him, he heard Rylee groan.

"I'm coming, baby," he whispered, gently moving the chair out of his path.

His eyes landed on the hoodie he'd placed beneath her when he delivered their son. It was now stained deep red with blood.

"You're awake," Xander said, dragging the chair closer. "Thank God."

She winced as she tried to sit up.

"I got you, I got you," he said low, helping her by the arm and adjusting the pillows behind her.

"What happened?" Her voice was hoarse, barely above a whisper.

Xander took a seat in the chair. "You almost gave me a heart attack is what happened, woman."

Her eyes left him, scanning the room. Rylee's hand flew to her stomach a second later.

"The baby," she gasped, pushing herself up. "Where's the baby?!"

"He's right there. Calm down, please, mama. *Please*," Xander told her, pointing. "He's asleep. He's good. Healthy. Ten fingers, ten toes. I counted twice."

He stood. "I'll get him."

As he lifted their sleeping son from the bassinet and placed him in Rylee's arms, he watched her face light up.

"Oh my God," she whispered. "Look at him." She looked up at Xander. "He's beautiful."

"Just like his mama," Xander said, one hand on her head, his eyes still on their boy. "We got an impatient son, for real. Junior wasn't tryna wait for shit."

Rylee laughed, then immediately winced, again.

"Take it easy," he advised. "Let me fix your pillow."

Xander was ready to do anything for her. Anything, except relive everything that had happened.

But somehow, he found the words.

He began retelling what happened, starting with the moment

she passed out—how he'd held their crying newborn in his arms, still wrapped in the towels and blankets they'd just bought.

He admitted he thought *he* might pass out too, just from the adrenaline.

Xander told her how the call for assistance got through, but the ambulance was delayed due to traffic.

"A police officer saw my truck parked on the shoulder," Xander said, taking her hand and kissing her fingers. "When he pulled up and stepped out of his cruiser, the color in his face drained to pure white."

Xander laughed nervously before taking a breath.

"He ran to his car, told me to follow behind him." Xander shook his head. "I had to get you in the truck while holding the baby—cord still attached. Like a scene out of a scary fucking movie."

"Oh, my God." Rylee pressed her hand to her chest.

"Yeah." He sighed. "I had the baby in one arm, the other gripping the steering wheel, weaving through traffic behind the cop." He ran a hand over his locs, that were tied back, that same hand then resting gently on their newborn in Rylee's arms.

"I had the heat blasting, wrapped him in a few of the towels and blankets from the baby store bag. Even with all that, I kept him tight against my chest, not wanting him to feel anything but me. I had no idea how it would turn out, but I just... I knew it *had* to work out."

Xander told Rylee how, once they arrived at the hospital, doctors gave her IV fluids, meds to stop the bleeding, and kept her under observation until she stabilized.

"They said you were hemorrhaging because of uterine atony."

Rylee looked down at their son, then over at him. "What's that?"

"Basically, your uterus didn't contract enough after delivery."

Rylee blinked, processing.

"So they gave you a fundal massage to stimulate your uterus," he explained, using his hand to demonstrate, "then Pitocin to help it contract. They were about to give you a blood transfusion, but they decided it wasn't necessary since you didn't lose too much blood... because I got you here in time."

He pressed a hand to her forehead. "But they're monitoring you. Checking vitals every hour, watching your blood count. But so far, baby, we're good. *You're* good. We got *so* lucky tonight. It could've ended *really* bad if we were out there any longer."

Rylee's eyes watered as she shook her head. "My God."

"You were amazing, Snoop." Xander smiled, inching his chair even closer. "*Amazing*. Through it all. I'm so proud of you."

"Me?" she rasped, her bottom lip trembling. "I'm proud of *you*. You delivered our baby, Xander. *You* were amazing. You saved my life."

Xander inhaled deeply, her words grounding him, anchoring him in the aftermath of the night.

His adrenaline had been pumping for hours, which was nothing new. He was used to high-pressure situations. The thudding pulse. The narrowed focus.

But never had it been for himself.

*Always* for someone else.

Now, so close to it all, his body still shaking beneath the surface, he was grateful. Unsteady, but here.

Rylee lifted her arm off the baby and gently wiped a tear from Xander's cheek with her thumb.

"Damn," he said low, sniffing twice. He leaned into her touch. "I ain't even know I was crying."

She smiled, her thumb still caressing his skin. "I love you so much, baby."

His eyes found hers, their gaze holding firm.

"*So* much," she whispered. "For the first time in my life, I am without words."

She smiled again, her smile reaching her eyes, softening them. "How the hell did I get this lucky to get someone like you?"

"A question I ask myself often about *you*." Xander leaned in, pressing his forehead to hers.

He kissed her there, then lowered to place a kiss on their son's forehead.

"Your parents and my mom are in the waiting room," he said quietly. "Nurses said they have to wait until visiting hours before they can see you or Junior... but they refused to leave. Said they'd just wait."

She giggled. "Of course they did."

"Your dad keeps trying to doctor his way in, but they have to keep reminding him this isn't his hospital."

Rylee snorted a laugh.

"I'm gonna go update them," he said, pressing another kiss to her forehead. "Then I'll be back to take the baby so you can get some sleep, okay?"

"Okay," she whispered, eyes dropping to Junior.

Xander nodded and turned to walk out.

He paused when she added, "We did it, Xander."

He turned to look back at her.

"I can't *believe* he's here," she said softly, stroking the baby's cheek.

"Yeah," Xander whispered to himself, his heart so full at the sight of Rylee and their son, alive and well. Here and breathing. "Same, Snoop. Same."

# eighteen

## RYLEE

RYLEE STEPPED out of the en suite, then quickly reentered to switch off the lights.

She'd only been in the house for few days and was still learning the little things, like how the light switch was to her right and not her left like in the brownstone.

Two months after giving birth to her third child, Rylee was officially in Greene Gardens, in the home Xander bought for their family.

Though she and Xander arranged for a moving company to relocate most of the things from the brownstone to Greene Gardens, a bulk of it remained in Brooklyn.

Xander insisted they leave it there and purchase new furniture. The plan was to keep the brownstone furnished for whenever they wanted to spend time in Brooklyn.

Rylee was grateful she didn't have to sell the brownstone. Grateful it hadn't even been a thought for Xander.

*"Of course you don't have to sell, Snoop," he'd said, caressing her cheek one night in bed.*

*The topic came up when she mentioned what she'd been thinking about doing with the brownstone once they moved into the house in Greene Gardens.*

*"This brownstone is yours, baby," he added. "The house in Greene Gardens is ours. There's no need to get rid of anything."*

*Rylee smiled with relief, the tension she'd been carrying in her shoulders finally settling.*

*"This place." He glanced around them, "This brownstone is where the kids grew up. It wouldn't be fair to uproot them and get rid of their childhood home. That wouldn't be right."*

And though she loved the idea of still having the brownstone, Rylee was making a home in Greene Gardens.

She'd taken a few walks with the baby since they arrived, familiarizing herself with the new neighborhood and the main strip of the village.

She even linked up with Ivy Pressman, one of her grief support group members who now called Greene Gardens home.

*"It's cute, right?" Ivy asked, adjusting the stroller her adopted son Levi slept in to make room for café patrons walking by. "This place is like a staple in my day."*

*Rylee didn't waste time reconnecting with Ivy. She'd just moved into the house officially a few days prior but wanted Ivy to show her around.*

*So she left the kids with Xander—who insisted she go—and met up with Ivy, who had just returned to Greene Gardens from the city after a mommy-and-me meet-up with Levi.*

*They settled on a quaint coffee shop on the main strip in Greene Gardens. The terrace overlooked the water. It was cold outside, so the terrace had heated lamps in every corner, making it feel warmer than it actually was.*

*"I like it." Rylee nodded, her eyes moving around them. "I really like it here."*

*"You haven't seen anything yet." Ivy winked. "But you know I got you."*

*"It's just so new." Rylee sighed. "All I know is Brooklyn."*

*"Girl," Ivy said, nodding in agreement. "Same. When I found out I'd have to make this place my new home, I swore I thought I'd die from boredom. When I moved out here, cafés like this weren't*

*even built yet. But now? I don't go any further than here. No need to."*

*"Yeah." Rylee smiled. A smile that came so easy. "I think I'm starting to feel the same way."*

At home, Rylee made her way to the side of the bed and lowered herself onto the carpet. On the floor were combs, hair ties, and a spray bottle filled with water.

With the children winding down for bed and Junior asleep in the bassinet she kept in her and Xander's room—coincidentally in the exact spot where her water had broken—Rylee decided it was time to finally tackle the one thing she'd been putting off.

Taking down her braids.

Her mother was set to arrive tomorrow to wash and style Rylee's hair.

Though she would've loved for her mother to install a new set of braids, Rylee already knew she wouldn't. Claudia would tell her to let her hair breathe between braided styles.

Claudia had promised to drive out to Greene Gardens once a week once the braids were down, to wash and restyle Rylee's hair in between. Anything to help her as a new mom of three.

Everyone was pitching in that way. In their own way.

That night, the room was quiet. The house was quiet. Soft light from the street lamp filtered in from outside. The neighborhood was quiet too, a sharp contrast to life in Brooklyn.

A lot of things were different here—something Rylee realized on her second night in Greene Gardens, sitting outside in the backyard.

*Her eyes traveled the sparse grass in the yard. It was after ten at night. The children, including the baby, were asleep, giving her time to herself.*

*Xander had just finished cleaning the kitchen when he stepped out to the backyard to join her.*

*"You like this part of the house the most, huh?"*

*Xander's voice behind her pulled Rylee out of her daze.*

*"This is your second night escaping out here."*

*Rylee snickered.*

*She'd been caught up in thought, imagining all the things she wanted to set up back there. A swing set. A trampoline.*

*His voice cutting through her vision pulled her back to now.*

*She turned toward him.*

*"I'm just making sure I enjoy my surprise purchase to the fullest. It's not every day a girl gets surprised with a whole house."*

*He parted his lips, then closed them, shaking his head as he relaxed into the chaise beside her.*

*"I bought a house without speaking to you first."*

*She smirked. "You bought a big ass house without speaking to me first."*

*He smiled coyly, the expression on his face making Rylee want to lean in and press a kiss to his lips.*

*Xander ran his hand over his locs and turned more to face her, taking her hands and holding them in his for a moment.*

*"I know we never really talked about how I went about buying the house... but I want to explain why I did it in that way."*

*"Xander—"*

*"Nah, please," he interjected, lifting her hands to kiss one at a time. "Let me. You deserve that."*

*Rylee fixed her eyes onto him.*

*"Because I don't want you thinking that your objections or feelings weren't considered, because they were."*

*Xander sighed, scooting to the edge of his seat.*

*"I went through the whole buying process in secret not because I'm a secretive person," he explained. "I was just worried you'd talk yourself out of wanting more when you deserved it."*

*Rylee blinked in response.*

*"You're my life now, Snoop," he told her, attention completely on her. "And I thought if I didn't just get the process started and get it done, it might never happen. Buying the house was my way of showing you what I saw in our future."*

*And somehow, even though she hadn't seen it then, she saw it now... clearly. In every wall, every room, and every quiet moment like this.*

*"I know," Rylee said, nodding. "I know that now. And I think my ther-apist Liz knew it too somehow, because she insisted I see the house... to see what you saw. Granted, she told my ass to wait until after Junior arrived, but you know... seems me and our baby boy being a little impulsive is something we have in common, I guess."*

*Rylee winked and Xander laughed, lowering his voice when his humor echoed around them.*

*"I just..." Xander ran his thumb over the back of Rylee's hand. "I want you to know that buying the house and only telling you after wasn't just about surprising you. It wasn't about replacing what you had, either. But you know, I also wanted to build something new for us too... and not just ask you to."*

*Rylee lifted her hand to caress the side of Xander's face. "Aww, baby."*

*Xander turned his head to press a kiss to her palm, taking her hand in his again.*

*"But look, I promise to run everything by you before I go through with it, moving forward. Promise."*

*Rylee shook her head. "Xander, that's not necessary—"*

*"It is," he cut in. "It so is, because although I'm so grateful you're here... that we're here... I want you to know your voice matters. Your feel-ings matter, and I'm always listening."*

Xander had been true to his word. What he didn't know is that Rylee had fallen so deeply in love with the house, she could not remember not wanting to be there.

Especially with Junior sleeping soundly just a few feet away in his bassinet... peaceful, safe.

His nursery was the most put-together room in the house, but like Nova and LJ before him, Rylee kept him close in these early months.

Some routines never change, even when everything else does.

She once heard that every pregnancy was different, and things were definitely different. From the birth to how much calmer Junior was compared to Nova and LJ.

Rylee felt more supported now than ever, having Xander around, making it a priority for her not to carry all the weight on her own.

Rylee settled into her seat on the carpet and got to work, singling out one of her braids and undoing it.

She smiled as she slid her fingers down the plait, feeling it unravel beneath her touch.

Her braids were the usual feel against her hand, but life was different now... and it was starting to feel so real. Like it finally belonged to her.

She honestly couldn't believe how hesitant she'd been about starting a life in Greene Gardens. Especially with how beautiful it was. How peaceful it was in the village.

There was something healing in moving there. Something she couldn't deny.

She smiled at the faint sound of Nova and LJ in the other room. Their chorus of laughter wasn't too loud, but audible enough to hear in her bedroom.

While the old her would've been worried about them waking the baby, she totally understood what her mother meant years ago when she told Rylee a baby should be able to sleep through an earthquake.

Xander stepped into the room, closing the door behind him.

"Got them to settle down with a few super slams."

Xander made a flipping gesture with his arms, then held one arm up in a flex. "They knocked out for the night."

Rylee snorted to herself.

Xander had gotten the kids into wrestling, watching old videos from the 90s when WWE was still WWF. Nova was the most obsessed and loved reenacting wrestling matches in her very spacious bedroom.

Xander approached the bassinet and leaned in to press a kiss to Junior's forehead.

"*Aht!*" Rylee said softly. "You wake him up, and he's yours for the night."

Xander straightened, resting a hand gently against Junior's head as he slept.

"Your pops will gladly stay up with you *all* night, little guy," he whispered, eyes locked on his son. "Ain't that right? *Mmm-hmm...*"

Rylee smiled at the sight of them. Xander in dad mode would always be her favorite thing to watch.

"LJ and Nova better not look to me to do any of that wrestling stuff with them," she joked. "I can barely carry myself with all this baby weight."

"*Aw,* baby," he said, getting on the floor in front of her and moving in for a kiss. "I love this weight on you. You look good, girl."

She snickered, then swallowed the last of her humor in an attempt to keep it down.

Xander's eyes moved to her braids. "What you got going on here? You should be sleeping when the baby's sleeping, mama."

Xander had been great and an excellent partner. Taking turns with Rylee to get up and tend to the baby at night, even after he completed 24-hour shifts in Brooklyn. He took off three weeks after the birth to be home with Rylee and Junior and was true to his word when he said this would be the easiest time for her compared to the others.

She smiled tiredly, feeling the burn in her eyes, but reasoning she'd get through it.

"I waited too long to take these out." She shrugged, removing the braiding hair and adding it to the growing pile by her thigh. "My mama is driving out here tomorrow to do my hair and I want to be ready for her."

He nodded. "Aight, slide over then and I'll help you out."

She laughed. "Baby, what you know about taking braids down?"

"Nothing." He took a seat behind her and moved her in front of him, between his splayed legs. "But how hard can it be?" He pressed a kiss to her neck. "Plus, you know I'll do anything for my baby."

She giggled as she positioned herself in front of him and Xander went right to work, singling out a braid just as Rylee did, and undoing it with ease behind her.

She smiled to herself as he removed one braid, then another.

"What's this spray bottle for?"

"To wet the hair and get the buildup out," she answered. "My mother will get the rest when she washes it tomorrow."

"Cool." He extended his hand for it. "Send it back here."

Rylee did as requested, smiling to herself as she worked, finding it hard to stay composed at how excited she felt in that moment.

It was more than Xander helping her with her hair. It was that there was nothing he ever felt he couldn't do, especially if Rylee needed it.

She still wasn't over him delivering their son.

She'd known Xander the man, but to see how he handled himself in a crisis?

It just did something so good to her.

Rylee was more in love with him than she ever had been.

He whistled as he pinched and removed the undone braiding hair from Rylee's strand of natural hair. "Baby, your hair is mad long, huh?"

"Because I don't do anything with it," she said with a giggle. "I'd slap those braids back on if my mother would let me."

He chuckled, his voice traveling around the room.

"*Shh,*" she shushed, her eyes moving to the bassinet. "You're gonna wake the baby."

Xander kissed the back of her neck, and his lips on her sent a chill down her back.

He pressed another kiss to her shoulder and left his lips there.

They sat there for a moment, in silence, Xander's arms wrapping around her waist briefly.

"This is *exactly* what I imagined when I closed on this house."

Rylee said nothing, just continued listening.

"Maybe not here taking my woman's braids out..."

She released a soft laugh.

"But here, together," he clarified. "Comfortable, enjoying each other's company. Kids comfortable in their rooms, baby boy asleep in *his* crib in *his* room... but we're still working on that portion of the vision."

Rylee smiled, turning to look at him over her shoulder.

He leaned in close and kissed her, letting his lips linger there as he wrapped his arm even tighter around her waist.

"Damn I'm lucky," he said on her lips before kissing her again. "I'd hate my guts if I wasn't me."

Rylee snorted a laugh and turned in her seat to face him, moving to his lap and straddling him.

"The only thing missing now," he added. "Is a wedding band under that diamond rock on your left finger."

Rylee smiled, wrapping her arms around the back of his neck.

He licked his lips, sliding her closer. "But I'm sure we can do something about that."

"*Mmm-hmm,*" Rylee said with a nod, moving in closer to peck him once, then twice, parting his lips with hers.

And for the first time, in her life, Rylee wasn't chasing away doubts and worries.

She was simply enjoying peace.

What a journey it had been—through grief, hesitation, and hard choices—all leading here... a new chapter in a new corner of New York.

Her children were happy.

Xander was too, as he so deserved.

And Rylee... she was finally beginning to see this place as her sanctuary.

She wasn't just surviving anymore.

She was living.

Greene Gardens wasn't just a fresh start. It was their home now.

Nova already had a favorite reading nook by the window, and LJ had claimed the garage for his science projects.

They had found comfort in the new and were evolving. Healing.

Rylee hadn't forgotten Lennox, like she feared.

And she never would.

This new life didn't feel like it was erasing him...

It felt like it was honoring what he'd taught her about love.

And Xander... he had made a home in Rylee's world. Not as a replacement for Lennox, but as something new.

Something that was hers.

Her peace.

Her partner.

Her next chapter.

One she was finally ready to step into, fearlessly.

*epilogue*

## XANDER

"XANDER," the officiant, Reverend Kareem Holden, said to Xander with a grin. "Whenever you're ready."

Xander nodded his understanding, his eyes returning to Rylee.

The two stood out in their backyard in Greene Gardens beneath a beautiful arching arbor formed by red and white roses. He held her hand in his, his grip tight but loving.

She stood on sparkling silver heels wearing a cream A-line dress that highlighted her curves and accentuated her shoulders in lace sleeves. Her hair, styled by her mother, was cornrowed in the front, her long curls loose and flowing along her shoulders.

Xander had found it hard to keep his eyes off her since she made it down the aisle to him.

It was their wedding day... one Xander imagined the moment he slid that diamond ring onto her finger, now winking in the late afternoon sun.

"Rylee," he started, needing to clear his throat to clear it of the heavy emotions that weighed it down. "Not long ago, we moved into this house and I thought that the moment was our version of complete. But it's here, right now, standing in front of you that feels more like the perfect completion and a beginning I can't wait to be fully inside of."

They'd only given themselves six months to plan. It was after a night out in Manhattan with no kids and hours to enjoy alone, just the two of them. They had just hit up their favorite taco truck and were making their way down the city blocks, headed for Xander's truck, when Rylee blurted, "Let's just get married later this year."

*The two had been going back and forth with ideas on the idea of a small versus big wedding. Neither of them wanted the fanfare. They wanted something simple. An event where they could invite only the people they loved and truly knew.*

*Xander threw an arm over Rylee's shoulder and asked, "What venue could we find that we wouldn't have to book a year in advance, Snoop?"*

*She smiled up at him, her beautiful eyes sparkling, making him smile back. "The backyard."*

That night, when they returned home, the two toasted to the decision with sparkling ginger ale in champagne glasses—since Rylee was nursing—and got to work planning the small event they now stood in the center of.

"The way you came into my world and turned it upside down in the best way." He shook his head, smiling, eyes only on her. "Only you could do that, baby. Only you could make the man who never thought past what the day offered, open himself to a world so big, so full of love and light."

Rylee's smile grew grand, revealing a toothy grin.

"You, Nova, LJ, and Junior," Xander continued, his eyes moving to his other favorite people. "Y'all gave me purpose. Something to look forward to. Something to love outside of myself, but that I quickly considered an extension of me. Y'all are my family, my heart. And you, Rylee?" He swallowed back the tears welling in his eyes. "You're one of the greatest things to ever happen to me. Only second to our boy who wouldn't be here if it weren't for you... so I guess that moves you up in rank to becoming the greatest. Congrats."

Everyone expressed humor around them, including Rylee.

"From the moment I stepped into your world, I felt it..." He nodded. "You were home for me. And that's when everything became clear... I'd be good anywhere, as long as I'm with you."

Though they'd done well with making the Greene Gardens house a safe haven they all looked forward to coming back to, it was at the insistence of Xander to keep the brownstone and not sell.

*"It'll be cool for us to go there when we want to get away from perfect."* *He grinned. "Have a vacation in Brooklyn."*

Though they all still saw Brooklyn throughout the week—Xander still worked at the firehouse in Park Slope and the kids were still enrolled in their schools in Brooklyn Heights—their time was limited in their home city. So, Xander reasoned the brownstone could be their escape whenever Rylee and the kids became homesick.

"Rylee, I promise to be the calm when life gets chaotic." He held her hand tighter, nodding to seal his words.

Xander's eyes darted between Rylee's, his heart full, his pulse steady.

None of this made him nervous. Not the uncertainty of the future. Not the feeling that he could never be enough for her.

The journey they'd been on was proof enough that their life together was fated. And her life before him was destined because of that.

"I promise to honor your story," he continued. "Even the chapters I didn't write."

Rylee closed her eyes, sniffed back tears.

Xander pressed a hand to her cheek and felt warmth rush through him when she leaned into his touch, resting her head in his hand.

"I vow to kiss you slow," he added, caressing her skin. "And fold the laundry fast because I know you run a tight ship around here, and you *mad* strict mama. But I respect it."

Rylee snorted, playfully tapping his chest. As expected, their family and friends joined in with a laugh of their own.

"Most of all, I promise to raise our kids like they're my heartbeat."

He threw a glance at Nova and LJ, then at Junior, who sat on the lap of Xander's smiling mother. "Because they are."

When he looked in that direction, he caught sight of the empty chair beside The Walkers—the one that bore their son, Lennox's name on a card propped up on the cushion.

Xander smiled at it with acknowledgment, respect, and understanding. Finally.

Life for Xander had been one he hadn't expected or really planned for. And it was that—that unpredictability—that made him excited to live it these days.

He had the woman. The great kids. The career and the friends to boost.

Life was officially great... and for him, he was just getting warmed up.

"I vow to keep choosing you, Snoop," he recited, refocusing on her and giving her a wink. "Even on the hard days, the quiet days, and the days when choosing means learning how to love you better."

Xander pinched her chin, running his thumb lovingly down the center.

"I may not be your first chapter... but I plan on being your favorite one."

* * *

RYLEE

"Rylee," Reverend Holden said, smiling and nodding toward her. "Your go."

Rylee snickered, moving her attention off the reverend and over to her soon-to-be husband, Xander, who stood before her dressed in the finest cream tuxedo. The top button of his dress shirt was undone. He was the finest husband she ever did see.

A husband.

The idea sent a charge through her that settled in her heart and made her force in a breath to keep the tears in.

Her friends Nadia and Parker had helped with her makeup, insisting they had to do something since Rylee refused to have bridesmaids. According to her, she was not going to piss either one of them off by not making them maid of honor.

In her bedroom, they took turns making their friend up, both Nadia and Parker dabbing at their eyes and smiling from the application of primer to the spritz of finishing spray.

*"You've given me hope, friend," Parker said. "I may need to stop mean-mugging these fools who approach me and give them a shot. See something for a little."*

*"For real," Nadia added, taking a seat on Rylee's bed and staring at her in awe. "Maybe I might keep my profile up on HeartMates—"*

*"Delete it," both Rylee and Parker instructed, turning to each other and laughing.*

*"Aht!" Nadia said over their humor. "Not y'all dogging the company I still work for! You know what, fuck y'all."*

*Rylee fell back in her chair, laughing even harder.*

It was the laughter Rylee needed before one of the biggest steps of her life.

She'd been taking a lot of big steps in her life. Moving out of the brownstone and now getting married. And each phase had felt like smooth sailing, because the decision was intentional, and now... she was open to it all, with wide open arms.

"Xander," Rylee started, tilting her head back to meet his eyes. "When I tell you I *never* thought I'd get here... that's an understatement. But I've come to learn whenever you're involved, you make the impossible possible."

Xander licked his lips, the corners pulled up into a smile.

"You met me at a time when I was still so sad," she voiced, her bottom lip quivering. "I'd experienced a loss that broke me in a way I never knew was possible."

Rylee glanced over at the chair that was open beside a smiling Ivy and Cyrus Walker, her eyes settling on the card with Lennox's name scripted, her heart swelling at the sight of it.

She knew if he were there, sitting in that chair, his smile would be so big.

*You finally got it right, Ry*, she could hear Lennox saying in her ear. And that brought a smile to her face.

"Through you, I've learned that grief doesn't vanish. It just... softens. And it only softens when you've found a soft place to land."

Rylee squeezed Xander's hand and sniffed back her tears.

"Xander, you are my soft place. From the day we met outside your mother's daycare, you have *always* been my soft place. And I can only pray I can be that for you too."

When she suggested they just get married in their backyard, she shocked herself. Rylee had always wanted marriage, and the end of her engagement years ago could have ruined that hope for her... which she believed it did.

But she learned that the right person will make you change your mind about decisions you thought were set in stone.

She also learned that the right person could make her want to stop trying to carry Lennox in her arms... and start learning how to carry him in her heart.

"Before you, I didn't know if I'd get here... standing in front of someone again with this much love in my heart, and this much excitement for the future. *Our* future."

She watched Xander's eyes water, him twisting his lips from left to right to keep the tears in.

"I love you *so* much that saying it to you every time charges me in a way that just agrees with every part of me."

Xander moved his eyes off her and turned a little to swipe a hand down his face.

"*Please*, baby, don't make me cry in front of these people," Xander joked. "They will *never* let me live it down."

Everyone laughed.

Rylee giggled, stepping closer to him to lay a hand to his chest.

Life had been amazing with Xander by her side. And although he'd been there for three years before all of this, her being able to accept it became like food to her soul.

No more did she resist. In fact, she'd woven her being so tightly with his, the idea that she wasn't once this close felt like a distant past.

"Xander, I promise to love you without hesitation, because you deserve more than that," she said. "And I promise to trust you without fear."

He smiled.

"To show up, speak up, and soften when it's easier to shut down... because you give me every reason to be soft in your presence. And I am more than confident you know what to do with *all* that."

"And do," he said, making her laugh.

"I vow to hold your hand and your heart... especially when the world tries to make you feel like you have to carry it all alone. You don't."

He nodded.

"'Cause you got me, and I got you," she recited his line back to him. "So we got us."

He balled his lips, but gave into the pull at his mouth and nodded, his smile so big beneath it all.

"And with that, I promise to make this house of ours a home you never want to leave, even on the hard days."

They'd already made their house a home full of love and comfort. And even though Xander insisted they keep the brownstone and visit it here and there, the children had already chosen what they felt was their haven.

She remembered the exact moment that showed her just how far they'd come.

A moment that had broken her heart in the quietest of ways...

*"Mommy?" Nova called as she approached Rylee's bedroom door in the brownstone.*

*Rylee was sitting on the bed, reading a book. This was one of the rare moments she was able to have to herself. Junior was asleep in the spare bassinet by her bed. The children had been busy in their rooms.*

*Well, at least they were before Nova came stepping inside.*

*"What's up, baby?"*

*Nova climbed her little frame onto the bed, folding her legs once she was comfortable in her seat.*

*"When are we going home?" she asked. "I miss my room so much."*

*The question hit Rylee square in the chest and made her close her book.*

*Her first inclination was to respond with, What are you talking about, Nova? We are home.*

*But she couldn't.*

*Her goal when they moved to Greene Gardens had been to get the children comfortable with their new environment. She'd planned several trips around the village to familiarize them with the area. But most of that had proven unnecessary.*

*It only took one night for both Nova and LJ to become acclimated with their new home. They were in love with their rooms, and had already created tight-knit bonds with the neighborhood kids.*

*It was like the perfect magnetic click for them over there.*

*That didn't stop Nova's question from hurting.*

*It hurt Rylee a lot.*

*Her daddy bought that brownstone with her in mind. Before Nova was even born, Lennox had bought that place for her.*

*Rylee forced a smile to keep her bottom lip from trembling. To keep the tears from forming.*

*This was a good thing. A wonderful thing.*

*Nova kept her big, beautiful eyes—ones she shared with Rylee—locked on her mother's, making it that much harder for Rylee not to break down.*

*They'd literally just arrived four hours prior, with plans to spend the weekend before heading back.*

*Plans change.*

*"Tomorrow," Rylee assured with a nod. "We'll go home tomorrow."*

Some days were harder for Rylee. The grief, as she said, was still there... but softer. And when she looked into her kids' eyes, and into Xander's, the future always seemed to extend its warm, welcoming hand. And she felt so good when she took it, every time.

"You gave me a love that never tried to replace the one I lost. Instead... you became the love I didn't even know I deserved."

Xander's Adam's apple bobbed as he swallowed hard, his eyes welling again.

"I'm *so* in awe of you. So in love." Rylee's smile grew, a tear streaking her makeup, but she didn't care.

"I've never felt luckier than the day I said yes to this life with you."

It was like the world vanished around them.

Yes, they stood at the altar dressed in their wedding best—Rylee in a cream A-line dress with lace sleeves, roses etched along the fabric; Xander in the matching cream tux, no tie—but to Rylee, it was just Xander and her, on any day.

There, in their backyard, creating a core memory for just the two of them.

To her, he was the greatest choice she'd made. Only second to her children.

And for once... she wasn't trying to figure out what happens next.

She was excited to just be.

"By the power vested in me in the great state of New York," Reverend Holden voiced, smiling. "I now pronounce you husband and wife. Xander, you may kiss your beautiful bride."

Xander took Rylee by her hand and whispered, "Get your fine ass over here."

She laughed from deep in her chest, her head tipping back as he wrapped an arm around her waist. Lifting onto her toes, she cupped his cheek with one hand to steady herself.

The instant their lips touched... the moment felt slow and sacred.

Their friends and family celebrated behind them, but their voices were muted.

All Rylee heard was Xander's satisfying moan—the sound he

released as he pulled her even closer—and in that moment, she felt like honey in his arms.

And she allowed it. She let it all happen without resistance, without hesitation, and without feeling like the pain she'd experienced would simply vanish at the end of it all.

Because she learned in all of this...

Love doesn't erase loss.

It writes something new beside it...

If you let it.

She pulled back to meet Xander's eyes, and he moved in close again, brushing the tip of his nose with hers.

"I love you," Rylee whispered.

"Oh, baby." Xander smiled so big she could see his back teeth. "I *so* love you."

Rylee leaned in for another kiss... and into the life they'd built, full of light, laughter, and love that lasts.

"Ladies and gentlemen," Reverend Holden broadcasted beside them. "Please continue to put your hands together for Mr. and Mrs. Xander Cox!"

**THE END.**

*final words*

Dear Reader,

Thank you so much for reading *Here Comes Love*. This story was years in the making and has lived rent-free in my head since concluding *Last Comes Love*, so I am so happy and proud to have finally gotten it on page. I always knew that Rylee's story would continue. And although I knew it would be a challenge for both Rylee and readers to accept her moving on to a new love, I knew I had the perfect love for her and a love story that was earned and all hers.

Every book was written to get Rylee to here, and I personally loved her journey.

There were a few cameos in *Here Comes Love*, all there to serve a purpose. Had Rylee's journey not happened in *Last Comes Love*, Yusuf Baldwin's journey would not have happened in *When Life Gives You Sunsets*. And Ivy Pressman—even though she didn't lose a spouse to a brain aneurysm—found hope through attending Rylee's Hope Collective meeting. That hope helped her continue forward in her new life as the appointed guardian of her late best friend's newborn in *Raising Love*.

Speaking of Ivy and the cameos, I wanted the parallels to be clear there too, not only in Rylee finding love while still grieving the loss of her best friend, but also in the cameos. If you noticed, there were two Ivys and two Levis, both present to reflect the intersection of Rylee's new life with her old one. One of her biggest lessons was realizing that she would—and could—never be the woman she was when Lennox was still here. That version of her couldn't grow in the world she lives in now… as painful of a truth as that was for her to accept.

Pain, as I've learned, though unpleasant, can be a powerful teacher. In Rylee's case, it was for her too. She is one of my favorite FMCs because she's a character that has been battle-tested, just like the readers who read her story *Last Comes Love* and continued to explore other titles in my book world.

*Here Comes Love* closes out this era in my writing. As of this writing, this story closes out the final open series in my catalog, and it's fitting that it's a story with a character who appeared in the first story that changed the way I wrote, *Last Comes Love. Here Comes Love* does the job of showing how connected my book world is and how purposeful those connections are.

The theory of six degrees of separation is the theme behind every cameo in my book world, and *Here Comes Love* completes the first tier of those connections.

Now, onward…

Thank you so much for reading *Here Comes Love.* I hope it was just as enjoyable a read for you as it was for me penning every word. If you are new to my world, welcome. You're a Brookelynite now. For my readers who have been rocking with me from a book or many books ago, thank you so very much for your support. Whether it's you trusting my pen, name-dropping my name in rooms I have yet to enter, and or recommending my books to anyone who would hear about them, I thank you. This and many other things among the mentioned actions make me loyal to those who have been loyal to me. I do this for us. I write what I want to read and what I think you want to read too. Thank you, as always, for reading and loving my work.

See you at the end of my next book.

Love,
BK

# *acknowledgments*

A loving thank you to my amazing husband who is without a doubt one of my biggest supporters. Your support is worth its weight in gold. I love you. To my children, who share my time with my writing projects, thank you for challenging me every day, because through you I've learned the true meaning of, "love is kind, love is patient" 😌. Mommy loves you. A special thank you to my reading family and early supporters of my work. I have grown so much as a writer, and I love that you've been on this journey with me. I thank you for sticking beside me and growing with me. You all have embraced my brand of writing and I'm beyond appreciative of it. Shout out to the readers who have reached out to me to share your thoughts regarding my books. I thank you for keeping me motivated and excited to create new projects for you. When I write, I keep you in mind. Thank you for your support. It's my soul food.

# character cameos

*In the order they appeared **or** were mentioned in Here Comes Love. Links to all books listed below can be found at this link - https:// brookelynmosley.com/ebooks-paperbacks/*

### Liz Peters
*Last Comes Love*
*Ebb & Flow*
*Meant to Be*
*Envy*
*Gluttony*
*Sloth*

### Lennox Walker
*Last Comes Love*
*Greed*

### Yusuf Baldwin
*When Life Gives You Sunsets*

### Ivy Pressman

*Raising Love*

**Bryant Greene**
*Greed*
*Home Before Midnight*

**Levi Weston**
*Cali & Lee*
*My Only*

**Hassani Franklin**
*My First, My Last*
*My Only*

For a more comprehensive guide on these characters and plenty others who appear in my books across my book world, download my *Characters & Book Connections Guide* here - https://Book Hip.com/QLVKQAB

# book club questions

1.   How did your view of Rylee shift as you followed her emotional journey in Here Comes Love?

2.   What scene or moment in the story impacted you most emotionally, and why?

3.   What was one trait or quality you loved most about Xander?

4.   What are your thoughts on how Rylee handled her grief throughout the story?

5.   How did you interpret the tension Rylee felt between honoring Lennox's memory and embracing new love?

6.   What were your thoughts on the scene where Rylee gave birth in the truck? How did it make you feel?

7.   What's your interpretation of the house in Greene Gardens and what it symbolized for their family?

8.  Did any quotes or lines from the story stick with you? Which ones and why?

9.  What were your thoughts on Rylee's support system (Liz, her parents, her friends, etc.) throughout Here Comes Love?
10. If you could ask Rylee or Xander one question, what would it be?

*about the author*

Brookelyn Mosley is a captivating voice in the world of black romance literature. With a gift for weaving heartfelt narratives and steamy encounters, she invites readers on journeys of love, passion, and self-discovery. Through her compelling storytelling, Brookelyn celebrates the beauty of black love and explores the complexities of relationships with authenticity and depth. With over 60+ titles, her stories resonate with true-blue readers, touching hearts and inspiring conversations about love, identity, and resilience.

**Connect With Me Online!**

**Facebook:** http://facebook.com/brookelynmosley
**Facebook Reading Group:** Brookelynites Book Lounge
**Instagram:** @Brookelynmosley
**My Website:** BrookelynMosley.com
**My Readers Website:** BKBookLounge.com
**My Mailing List:** https://brookelynmosley.com/bk-insiders-club/